Death is Personal

SALLY DALLAS

CHAPTER ONE

Four deaths in four months is not a coincidence.

The morning of the first incident, the only one law enforcement classified as a murder, began like any other Tuesday. Pam Guerrero and her husband, John, awaken in their California King at 7:00 a.m. to the aroma of freshly brewed coffee. Their Mediterranean style, two-story home, is more spacious than they need, thus a coffee bar in the master bedroom is essential.

Pam peers through the sliding glass doors, over the wrought iron balusters of the balcony. Between the mini mansions, she catches a sliver of ocean view. She and her first husband, Steve, bought the stately home in the nineties, after they hit the equivalent of the lottery with a tech investment. They had gotten in on the ground floor of Qualcomm, now a global brand. Pam thought they sold their interest too cheap, but it still allowed them to live comfortably in the overpriced paradise of La Jolla, California.

Pam misses Steve. He was the love of her life. She's still mad at him for dying of leukemia at the age of fifty-five. They were going to see the world together. John doesn't like to travel.

The couple consume their liquid fuel while reading news on their iPads. The shrill blare of a siren interrupts their non-interaction.

"What was that!" Pam glares at John.

"I don't know." He shrugs, returning his focus to the news.

"Duke is barking big time!" Pam jumps out of bed, and flies down the stairs, rushing to the kitchen window. Peeking through the blinds, she sees a police car with lights flashing race past. She gives her labradoodle a reassuring pat on the head, before returning to the window.

John, shirtless and wearing plaid boxers, leisurely ascends the stairs. He's handsome, mid-sixties, with thick gray hair and a chiseled jawline. His face and arms are tanned from playing too much golf. Opening the sub-zero refrigerator, he examines the milk carton, searching for the expiration date. Breakfast is his priority. He could care less about the sirens.

"I think they're at Marvin and Beth's house!" Pam exclaims. "Call the station and find out what's going on."

"I'm not calling them." John states adamantly. "I don't work there anymore." He retired five years ago after a successful thirty-five-year career as an officer for the San Diego Police Department. "They won't tell me anything, anyway. And you need to stay out of it, Pam." He points his finger as though he's scolding a child.

An ambulance zooms by, followed by a van with a huge antenna on top and 'CBS News 8 San Diego' plastered on the side.

Ignoring John's warning, Pam slips on denim leggings and a floral tunic top and heads out the door to Beth's house, three doors down. Swinging her arms with a single-minded mission, she walks quickly down her cobblestone walkway to the sidewalk. The cool breeze blowing on her face is an effective substitute for her second cup of coffee. The tops of the palm trees are fluttering, and gray clouds dot the blue sky. She stops on the sidewalk, in front of the house next to the Marvin and Beth Fitzgerald's home, contemplating if she should proceed.

The ambulance is parked in the driveway, and the news vehicle is in the street. A news caster with long blonde hair, dressed in a pink pantsuit, is bossing around her cameraman. A police officer is standing in the driveway, arms intertwined across his chest, like a sentry standing guard. Pam sees the EMT's slamming the back doors of the ambulance as the siren begins blaring.

Pam's obsessive curiosity is a carryover from her days as an investigative reporter for the 'San Diego Evening Tribune'. She covered a sensational crime wherein a young girl was killed by her neighbor. It made national news, and an indelible impression on Pam's psyche.

Pam left her career fifteen years ago when journalism evolved to being opinion rather than fact. Pam now spends her time writing a travel blog, providing an insider's view of the local hot spots. She misses the challenge of discovering the who, what, where, and why of a newsworthy story.

Marvin and Beth moved into the upscale enclave five years ago. The couples became fast friends, and hang out about once a month to swim, barbeque, or play cards.

Pam returns home finding John eating cereal, and watching 'Good Morning America'.

"What's up?" He asks, with his gaze focused on the small television mounted on the wall opposite the breakfast table.

"I don't know." She sits next to him. "But I'm going to find out."

John shakes his head, knowing he can't argue with her

tenacity.

An hour later Pam steps out to the sidewalk, peering down the street to her friend's house. The commotion has subsided. The ambulance and news van are gone.

She walks past two beautiful homes of Spanish architecture, then up the stone paved walkway to the front door of Marvin and Beth's Mediterranean mini-mansion. The columns framing the entry are wrapped with yellow caution tape. Sliding under the barrier, Pam peeks in the window adjacent to the front door. She closes her fist and knocks with force. No answer. She rings the bell. Still no response. Disappointed, she returns home.

"Beth didn't answer the door." She announces to John, finding him upstairs getting dressed.

"It's none of your damn business, Pam. They'll tell us what happened when they're ready."

Two months ago, Pam and John's next-door neighbor had a break-in at their home. The intruder stole electronic devices, a few tools from the garage, and an Xbox. The unfortunate event prompted Pam to install 'Blink' surveillance cameras on the front porch and back patio. As the organizer, and self-appointed head of the 'Neighborhood Watch Program', she has tried to convince her neighbors to do the same. John believes community led organizations are a waste of time.

Pam's preoccupation with the safety of her neighbors, and writing her tourism blog, distract her from being married to a man she no longer loves. The fire that ignited them in their time of need is no longer being fueled. Passion has been replaced with apathy.

She retrieves her laptop from her office, and plants herself at the formal dining table, a space they only use on Thanksgiving and Christmas. The traditional table for eight is adorned with a centerpiece of fragrant vanilla candles and fake succulents that Beth helped Pam arrange.

John descends the stairs, dressed for golf in his khaki shorts and light-green polo shirt. He stops in route to the kitchen. "Why are you sitting in here?"

"I'm watching the street."

"You're obsessed." He takes a bottle of 'Perrier' out of the fridge. "I'm off to the course." He shouts to Pam as he exits through the garage, without so much as a goodbye kiss.

Pam stares out the window, while intermittently writing her latest blog post. The hours slip by. At about 3:00 p.m., Beth's Audi cruises past. Pam slides on her sandals, then bolts out the door. She walks quickly down the block, slowing her pace as she ascends Beth's walkway.

There's a black and white parked in the driveway, next to Beth's car. *How did that police car get past me? This is a cul-de-sac, only one-way in.*

Pam inhales deeply, then pounds on the door. A burly policeman in a crisp, navy-blue uniform opens it, staring at her in silence.

"Hello, I'm Pam. I live a few houses down." She points to the left. "I'm here to visit my friend, Beth Fitzgerald."

"Now is not an appropriate time, Ma'am." He closes the door in her face.

She rings the bell and waves at the 'Ring' camera; cognizant she's being filmed.

The door opens, again. "Ma'am, I told you, this is not a good time." He snaps.

Beth walks up behind him. Her hazel eyes are bloodshot, and charcoal streaks of mascara stripe her flushed cheeks. She's still beautiful in her green pantsuit with her thick auburn hair pulled to one side.

"Oh, Pam." She sobs. The officer steps to the side.

"Beth, dear, what's going on?" Pam pleads

"Marvin is gone." She wipes her cheek with a tissue.

Pam covers her mouth with her hands. "I'm so sorry." Sympathetic moisture wells in her eyes. "What happened?"

The policeman begins closing the door, again.

"We'll talk later." Beth says, sniffling.

"Please, call me when you can." Pam squeezes in her comment before the door closes.

Pam goes home and cleans the refrigerator - a fruitless attempt at distraction. Marvin and Beth are dominating her thoughts. She so enjoys their company. Marvin always wins their bridge games. He is awkward, yet witty. A perfect balance to Beth's faux sophistication. Ruminating about how Marvin could have died is driving her crazy.

She calls John to tell him Marvin passed, although she's unaware of the details. He sounds irritated that she interrupted his golf game.

John and Pam married nine years ago, after a whirlwind, six-month romance. They met at a cancer support group when her husband, and his wife, were both going through treatment. Their spouses died within a month of each other. Being caregivers was about all they had in common. And being vulnerable. And lonely. Pam fell for his confidence and good-looks. She was blind to his arrogance and self-centeredness. John's charm wore off soon after they got married.

John isn't stupid. He recognized Pam was a good catch from the moment they met. She was a Charger's cheerleader back in the day, and that fascinated him. She has flawless skin, and her long gray hair is the shade young women pay a fortune to achieve. The most alluring feature - her money. She has lots of it, and only one daughter to complicate their lives, and Jill was already married and living in Texas.

Returning from his golf game, John finds his wife in the

kitchen cleaning out the junk drawer. He was hoping she had started dinner, but there is no aroma of a meal in progress.

"Are you okay?" He asks, knowing she cleans fanatically when she's stressed.

"I can't believe Marvin is dead."

John wraps a consoling arm around her shoulders. Pam relaxes in his embrace as her eyes begin tearing.

"What happened?" John asks.

"I don't know! There was a policeman at her house. He wouldn't let me talk to her."

"Well, it had to be the Parkinson's." John says with faux sympathy. "He's had it for a while."

"No." Pam shakes her head. "Something else is going on."

"Don't worry, Pam. Beth will tell you when she's ready to talk about it."

"No, that's not it. Something terrible has happened. I can feel it." She pats her chest with her open palm. "What is Beth going to do without Marvin?"

"She'll be okay." John utters reassuringly. "She's a strong businesswoman. She can handle whatever life throws at her."

"You're right, John." Pam hates admitting he's right. "She's a very capable woman."

While John goes upstairs to change his clothes, Pam nukes a frozen lasagna, and tosses a salad. They sit at the breakfast nook, watching television while eating their mediocre dinner. Pam nearly chokes on her pasta as the local anchor reports an unbelievable shocker:

"Retired UCSD professor, Marvin Fitzgerald, was the victim of a fatal stabbing in his La Jolla home. He was found early this morning by a home health care worker.

The homicide is under investigation."

An attractive photo of Marvin with his curly gray hair, wearing a green sweater, and wire rimmed glasses, flashes on the screen.

"What? Stabbed?" John turns to Pam. "Marvin had no enemies."

"This is terrible. Poor Marvin. And poor Beth. See, I told you something bad happened!" Pam punches John's upper arm with her fist. "How does one deal with something so horrific?"

The killing of Professor Marvin Fitzgerald was the first murder in the neighborhood, but not the last.

CHAPTER TWO

Pam's been waiting for a call from Beth for four days. Unable to quell her patience any longer, she walks to her friend's house.

Beth's son's 'Tesla' is in the driveway. Pam approaches the front door. After one ring, it opens slowly.

"Oh, Josh, I'm so sorry." Pam embraces Beth's son gently.

"Thanks." He forces a smile.

Beth walks up behind him. As Josh heads to the kitchen, she motions Pam to come into the foyer. Pam throws her arms around Beth's shoulders. They hug intensely, both sobbing quietly.

"I'm so sorry, Beth." Pam follows her into the living room. "Marvin will be terribly missed. Are you going to be okay?"

"I'm okay." Beth inhales deeply while wiping a tear from her cheek. She eases into the loveseat. Pam sits next to her, lovingly patting her knee.

"What happened?" Pam's eyes widen with intensity as she leans toward Beth.

"I was at a conference in Phoenix. I got a call from the SDPD telling me to catch the first flight to San Diego. They told me Marvin had been stabbed, and that he was in critical condition, but they didn't give me any details. When I got to the hospital, he had already died." She places her elbows on her knees, covering her face with her hands. "Oh, Pam, I didn't get a chance to tell him goodbye."

Pam gently sets her hand on top of Beth's. "Stabbed? How awful." Pam glances at a framed photo on the wall of Beth and Marvin in Hawaiian print clothes at a picturesque beach. "And unbelievable." She squeezes Beth's fingers.

"He was home alone. One of my employees, who was checking on him because I was out of town, found him in his study, hunched over his desk. He had five stab wounds in his back." She's weeping. Profuse tears stream down her cheeks. "The doctor said the incisions missed his heart. The trauma of the ordeal caused him to have a heart attack. That's what killed him."

"Do the authorities have any idea who could have done such a horrific act?" Pam asks.

"No clue." Beth shakes her head and stares at the Persian rug under their feet.

"Marvin was such a pussycat." Pam says. "Everybody loved him. He had no enemies, did he?"

"Not that I'm aware of." Beth pulls another tissue from the box on the wood inlaid end table. She dabs her tears.

"Was it a robbery gone wrong? Was there anything missing? You know the house next door to us was broken into a couple months ago? Was a window or door broken?"

"I don't think it was a break in. Nothing was missing. Marvin never locked the doors. He was so trusting. He felt safe in our home."

"Marvin loved you so much, Beth. You have been taking such wonderful care of him since his diagnosis."

"Not really." She stares at Pam somberly. "I work too much. I should have been here for him."

"Well, your employees fill in for you. They're professionals." Beth owns 'Sunset Health', the second largest health care placement agency in San Diego County.

"We're having a Celebration of Life at Mount Soledad Veteran's Memorial a week from today. Can you make it?"

"Of course. John and I will be there."

Pam was not aware Marvin was a veteran, but it makes sense since he collected military memorabilia. He had retired two years ago from a long career as a history professor at the University of California, San Diego. His expertise was medieval studies. He had a fascinating collection of ancient weapons in his study.

"Please, let us know if you need anything. John and I are here for you." They stand and embrace whole-heartedly.

Beth follows Pam to the door.

"Josh and his wife, and the boys, are staying here until after the service. They are very helpful. I'll be okay, Pam. Thank you for your concern."

The day of Marvin's celebration of life, gray clouds swirl over San Diego. The drizzle adds to the somber ambiance. The event is well attended by Marvin's relatives, his former colleagues at UCSD, old friends, and members of his Rotary Club. Josh delivers a heart-felt eulogy, honoring his father's life. Beth's demeanor is stoic and strong. *She's always so put together.* She speaks eloquently when she thanks everyone for sharing their diverse stories about Marvin, and for attending the service.

After the memorial, the attendees gather at the Fitzgerald home for wine and charcuterie trays poolside. John is chatting with Beth's daughter-in-law, and helping replenish the serving platters, wine glasses, and cleaning up. Pam notices, because he never does that at home when they have guests. He's excessively attentive to Beth, hugging her often. A tinge of jealousy crawls up Pam's spine. *What am I thinking? She's just lost her husband, she needs consoling.* John is proficient at turning on the charm when he chooses. He just chooses not to with Pam anymore.

Three days later, Pam is at Beth's doorstep at 9:30 a.m. with a plate of blueberry muffins, fresh out of the oven. She rings the bell. No answer. As she descends the walkway to return home, the creaking sound of the door opening behind her coaxes her to turn around.

"Pam? Did you need something?" Beth asks. She's haggard, with bags under her eyes and flat hair. Her wrinkles are more prominent without makeup. *She's been through hell.*

"Good morning, Beth." Pam smiles warmly, at a loss for the appropriate words to console her friend. "How are you doing?"

"Well, I'm tired. Josh and his wife, and the boys, left yesterday. I love my grandsons, but they're a handful."

"I hear you. I love spending time with my grandkids, but their activity level is exhausting."

"Oh, to be able to bottle that energy." Beth smiles weakly. "Would you like a cup of coffee?"

Pam nods and follows her into the foyer, past the dining room with its wood beamed ceiling and massive table, through the roomy kitchen, to the bay-windowed breakfast nook. They sit at the table, coffee mugs in hand, gazing at the teal blue pool surrounded by stone pavers that blend into the grass. Multi-colored roses overflow the retaining wall that lines the fence.

"Your yard is so beautiful, Beth."

"Marvin enjoyed gardening. He even liked pulling weeds, and mowing. I had to hire a gardener a few months ago. It just got to be too much for him with his Parkinson's. And he had started repainting the guest room, but never finished. I'm going to have to hire a painter."

"I'm not proficient with household repairs, but you know John is. He can help you, or at least give you some direction on a contractor to hire."

"Thanks, Pam. I'll take you up on that."

"Sorry to bug you. I'll admit, I'm obsessive sometimes. It drives John crazy. I thought of something, and I just must ask." Pam hesitates, broaching the subject with caution. "Your security cameras, do you get notifications on your phone when motion is detected?"

"I'm always too busy to mess with that stuff." Beth waves her hand in front of her face. "I think Marvin may have."

"What did the police find when they reviewed the footage?"

Beth pauses. "Um, well, apparently, they weren't working properly. They were going on and off. I think we may have had a power outage."

"So, the camera didn't capture video of the perpetrator?"

"I don't think so. At least the police didn't tell me it did." She delivers a blank stare.

"They would have told you, I'm sure. That's weird, we don't have power outages around here very often."

"I know, it's strange, isn't it?" Beth responds.

Pam stands, stretching her legs. "I remember, the first time John and I came over, right after you moved in, Marvin showed us his ancient weapons collection. He was very proud of it."

"Yes, he was. They're worth over a million." Her demeanor changes from pitiful to stoic. "I hate them. To me they represent death."

"Can I see his collection again?"

"I guess so." Beth shrugs, then reluctantly agrees.

Pam trails her into the study, a spacious, wood paneled room that could use more light. To the left, behind Marvin's massive mahogany desk, are bookcases filled with books. Along the back wall, French doors open to their lush, green lawn and picturesque pool. The right wall displays multiple swords and ancient weapons, hung with precision. Below the swords is a glass case with knives and daggers lined up in an order that is indiscernible to Pam.

Her eyes follow the top row, and then the second one.

The label 'Cinquedea' catches her eye, because there is no corresponding weapon above the label. It's gone.

"It appears one is missing." Pam points to the empty spot in the case.

"The detective noticed that, too. He asked me if Marvin took it out. I couldn't remember. And he asked if he regularly removed his knives, for cleaning, or to admire them. I told him that once a collectible went into the display box, it stayed there forever."

Pam detects a key hole below the metal edge, in the middle of the case. She instinctively tries to lift the long glass lid.

"It's locked." Pam says, glancing at Beth.

"Yeah, Marvin kept it locked. I don't even know where the key is." She responds nonchalantly.

"Does the detective think the missing weapon was the one used to stab Marvin?"

Beth hesitates, gazing out the French doors to the serene pool, then returns her focus to Pam. "Evidently, he does."

"Have they found it?"

"Not yet." Beth declares curtly. "But I assume they're looking. I'm not at all pleased with the progress of the San Diego police department so far. Or I should say, lack thereof."

Pam stares at Beth in puzzlement. Her thoughts are racing. *Without a murder weapon, and no surveillance footage, how can law enforcement even attempt to find Marvin's killer?*

CHAPTER THREE

Three weeks after Marvin's murder, another unexpected death occurs in the neighborhood.

As their having their morning coffee in bed, Pam reads the online obituaries, a habit she developed after her first husband died. She recognizes the name, and photo, of their neighbor, Richard Johnson.

"John, Mr. Johnson, who lives on the next street over, died. I just read it in the obituaries." Pam seizes John's arm, commanding his attention. "He was only seventy."

"Who?" He looks up from his iPad.

"Richard Johnson. I chat with him when I'm walking Duke. I saw him last week. We talked about the 'Neighborhood Watch Program', and Marvin's murder. We were discussing pros and cons of different surveillance systems. They have a 'Ring'."

"How do you remember that?"

"Unlike you, I actually listen to what people say."

"I don't know him," he says, eyes glued to his device.

"You'd recognize him if you saw him. I didn't realize he was even sick. He was so active and spry. He didn't seem seventy. I need to bring his wife a casserole. Or a pie."

"Spare her your casserole." John flashes a sarcastic grin.

He leaves for his golf game while Pam rummages through the pantry, trying to locate the ingredients for a pie. She finds a bag of chocolate chips. *Who doesn't like chocolate chip cookies?* She whips up the batter and pops them in the oven.

While the treats are still warm, she places them on a decorative stoneware plate from her unmatched extras, and walks to the next block to make the delivery.

After one knock on Richard Johnson's door, it opens slowly. A slim, middle-aged woman stares at Pam, then gazes at the cookies, smiling reticently. Her overdone makeup is flawless. She's stylish in her red heels, tight floral dress, and long bleached-blonde hair. She looks about twenty years younger than Richard.

"Hello, I'm Pam. I live one block over. Are you Mr. Johnson's daughter?"

"Aren't you a sweetie." She smiles, flinging her long hair behind her shoulder. "I'm his wife." She clenches her teeth like she's posing too long for a photo.

"I'm so sorry to hear about Richard. I often ran into him when I was walking my dog."

"Please, come in. I'm Laura Johnson." Pam trails her into the living room and follows her lead, sitting on the gray linen sectional. The walls are adorned with abstract art prints, and every decorative item in the bookcase is positioned perfectly.

"These are for you." Pam places the plate of cookies on the glass coffee table.

"Thank you." Laura grabs a cookie and takes a bite.

"You have a beautiful home." Pam says admiring a painting.

"Thank you." Laura, mumbles. "The cookie is

delicious."

"Laura, I just saw Richard about a week ago. I know it's none of my business, but he was always so pleasant to me. And he seemed so healthy. I hope you don't mind that I ask. What happened?"

"Well, the doctor said he had an aneurysm." She declares matter-of-factly. Her attitude is aloof and unconcerned.

"How shocking." Pam's brows raise asymmetrically. "What kind of aneurysm?"

"There are different kinds? I'm not a doctor; I don't know the details." She twirls her hair, then glares at Pam. "I was out shopping with my friend. When I came home, he was lying on the couch. Honestly, I thought he was napping, but when I realized he wasn't breathing, I called his daughter. She's a nurse. She came over right away and confirmed he was already gone, so she called the funeral home." Her delivery is eerily void of emotion.

"Oh, I'm so sorry." Pam's eye brows converge sympathetically.

"The service is Monday at the Oak Hill Memorial Park in Escondido. You can come if you want to." She flings her hands as she's talking. "Tuesday I'm flying to Hawaii. I've got to get away to clear my head."

Her attitude is unconscionable. Pam wants to confiscate the cookies, and slap her. "I didn't mean to interrupt your day; I just wanted to express my condolences." Pam stands. "Pleasure to meet you, Laura." She says insincerely, as she steps toward the foyer.

"Yeah, you too." She follows Pam and opens the door for her. "Later." Laura's forgotten Pam's name already.

As Pam reaches the sidewalk, the roar of a muscle car reverberates in her ears. A black, late model, Camaro pulls into Laura Johnson's driveway. A muscular, middle-aged man with a shaved head and grayish goatee exits the vehicle. Staring Pam down through his mirrored sunglasses, he then turns and enters the Johnson house without knocking.

Pam goes home and searches Facebook and Instagram, finding posts of Laura Johnson with the Camaro driving stud. They're drinking wine, hot-tubbing, and hanging out at the Torrey Pines Country Club.

The second John walks in the door, Pam unloads her frustration. "Our neighbor, Laura Johnson, is a skank!"

"Who?" John flings off his Padres cap and sits in the leather recliner in the family room, He grabs the remote control.

"I found her photos on social media, and her husband Richard isn't in any of them! Laura Johnson told me she's going to Hawaii the day after his service. She's got to be going with her studly boyfriend. He showed up at her house after I left."

"Pam, take a chill pill," he says, removing his golf shoes.

"I don't like that woman. She's a gold-digging skank. Richard was the picture of health. How could he be alive one day and just die the next? Something is fishy."

John stares at her with a serios squint. "It's none of your business."

Pam's suspicions are right on target. Unbeknownst to Mr. Richard Johnson, he paid for his own demise.

CHAPTER FOUR

Four weeks later, another death occurs in the neighborhood.

Passing by the Johnson residence on her morning dog walking trek, Pam notices a 'For Sale' sign perched prominently on the front lawn.

Pam is curious to know if Laura has already moved. There are no vehicles parked in the long, hedge lined driveway. Stopping on the front landing, she waves at the security camera, as if she's on the red carpet. The blue light flashes. Guessing that it is a voice enabled system, she talks to the device.

"So, your house is for sale. Sorry to see you go." Then she peaks in the window. The furniture is arranged with precision, and the wood floor is dustless. The modern art work is still on the walls.

Pam is startled by a screeching siren. A fire engine speeds past, parking in front of a house down the street.

"Oh, my Gosh!" Pam talks to her labradoodle, as if Duke can respond. "Is there a fire?"

Pam paces quickly to the sidewalk, then heads in the direction of the fire truck. An ambulance races past, parking in the driveway of the two-story home just ahead.

She walks cautiously toward the chaos, stopping in front of the house next door to the commotion. The sirens are silent, but voices are shouting. Two buff firemen run out of the house to meet the ambulance. White coated paramedics pull a gurney out of the back of their vehicle and frantically push it up the driveway, into the garage. Across the street, Pam sees neighbors standing on their lawns, rubber necking the situation.

Moments later, the paramedics come barreling out of the house. They're wheeling a gurney carrying a petite woman with short gray hair. An oxygen mask covers her face, and her blouse is splattered with blood stains.

This can't be another murder! Not in my neighborhood.

A police car appears out of nowhere and parks in the street, uncomfortably close to where Pam is standing.

The officer exits the vehicle. He's a big man, in a tight uniform. "Please folks, go back inside," he shouts, waving his arm. "Nothing to see here."

"We better go home." Pam says to Duke.

Pam goes home to her empty house. *John is golfing again.*

She loads up on corn chips while watching her favorite soap opera. After eating too many, and feeling guilty, she hears the garage door open. She rushes to the kitchen as John enters.

"John, there was another death! I was walking Duke and a firetruck appeared out of nowhere, and then an ambulance."

"Who died?" John asks, as he casually tosses his cap on the breakfast nook table.

"I don't know!" She exclaims. "It was two blocks over. I'm going to find out."

John shakes his head. "Find out what?"

"Who died, and how?"

"It's none of your business, Pam." He glares at her, then goes into the family room and switches the channel from her show.

Pam works on her computer, avoiding John until dinner. She throws a frozen pizza into the oven, and tosses a chopped salad.

John munches his pizza in silence. Pam is glued to local news. There are no reports of any criminal activity in La Jolla.

The next night Pam cooks a real meal of chicken with sundried tomato cream sauce, fresh broccoli, and rice.

"This is delicious, Pam." John mumbles with his mouth full.

Pam ignores him. She watches the news attentively, waiting for the report of a violent crime in her neighborhood. No such accounting appears on the local news.

"Pam, a normal death doesn't make the evening news. You need to move on." John says.

"Normal death?" Pam flashes air quotes. "What's that supposed to mean?"

"Stop worrying so much about the neighbors." John says with a stern brow. "You care more about them than you do me."

"John, we could be next! There could be some serial killer out there, randomly doing away with people. Three deaths in three months is not a coincidence."

He glares at her as though she's an idiot. "Serial killers are very rare."

"I have to find out what happened to that woman. Maybe it's related to Marvin's killing, or Richard Johnson's death. And I talked to Beth last week. There has been zero progress in solving Marvin's murder. You need to call your old buddies at the department."

"Calm down, Pam. You're talking like a lunatic. It's always unfortunate when someone dies, but for you to think they're related is ridiculous." He stands abruptly, and takes his plate to the sink.

The next day, after John leaves for the golf course, Pam walks to the house where the incident occurred the prior week.

The oversized Mediterranean style home has overgrown bushes hiding its beauty. The paint is peeling on the chocolate brown fascia boards, and the picture windows facing the street are covered in water spots and cobwebs.

She knocks on the door, surveying the entry-way beams, searching for a security camera. She detects one, but it isn't familiar, like a 'Blink' or a 'Ring'.

The door creaks open. An old man with hunched shoulders, and a scruffy gray beard, wearing a wrinkled plaid shirt, answers. He stares at Pam in silence.

"Hello, I'm Pam Guerrero. I was walking my dog last week, and saw an ambulance at your house. I'm not being nosy, really, I'm not. I'm the head of the 'Neighborhood Watch Program'. I just want to be sure everything is okay."

"I know who you are," he mutters gruffly. "I recognize you from the photo on the Watch Facebook page."

"Oh, yes, that would be me. So, you're a Facebooker?"

"God, no." He shakes his head as he studies the floor. "My wife showed it to me."

"Do you have a moment to talk?"

"Maybe." He looks up. Pam perceives pain in his light blue eyes. "What do you want?" he asks in an angry tone.

"I'm just a concerned neighbor." Pam smiles warmly.

"Come in, I guess. I'm Stan Powalski." He extends his hand. It feels like sandpaper in Pam's overly moisturized palm.

Pam follows him into the kitchen. It's a mess with dishes piled high on the counters and pots and pans overflowing the sink. He sits in the ladderback chair, and takes a swig from his mug. Pam assumes it's coffee, although she detects the scent of whiskey. She takes the chair opposite him, moving a pile of mail to make room to rest her elbows.

"So, if you don't mind me asking, Stan, what happened last week?"

His bloodshot eyes fill with tears. "It was my wife."

"What about your wife?" Pam asks gingerly.

"She died." He states somberly, turning his gaze away from Pam to a collage of family photos plastered on the refrigerator.

"I'm so sorry." Pam places her hand on his arm to convey her condolences. "How long were you married?"

"Fifty-four years."

"Wow, that is awesome. I hope you don't mind me asking... what happened?"

He pulls his arm back. "I don't want to talk about it."

"I know we just met, but believe me, this conversation is confidential."

He stares at the refrigerator, again. "I wasn't home when it happened." Then he looks back at Pam. "I was at the VFW. I'm on the BBQ team. When we cook for events, I'll be gone all day. Well, from about ten in the morning until six." He pauses as though he's changed his mind about sharing the story.

"And?" Pam prompts. "Then what?"

"About an hour after I left, she got a gun out of the cabinet and shot herself in the chest. She sent me a text right before she did it."

"Oh, Stan, that is awful! What did the message say?"

"I love you. Goodbye." He rubs his bloodshot eyes and blows his nose. "She threatened to kill herself before, so I rushed home. There she was, lying on our bed with my gun in her hand, and a hole in her chest. I called 911, but I knew it was too late."

"I'm so sorry, Stan. Were the guns in a safe?"

"Yeah, but I didn't lock it. I'm old. I can't remember

the combination."

"Had she been depressed?"

"Well, yes. She's been suffering from depression for a long time. She's been on and off meds for years. She had good days and bad." He stares at the floor and wipes his tears with his sleeve. Then he touches my arm, and looks into my eyes. "My wife wouldn't kill herself." He pulls his arm back as though he's violated my personal space.

"You don't think so?" I say with sympathy.

"No way." He shakes his head. "At least not with a gun. She's way too chicken. She had never even fired the damn thing. I used to shoot it sometimes for target practice. I have a few handguns, and a rifle. She hated guns. She wouldn't even know how to load it. The police automatically assumed suicide, but I know it wasn't."

"But she sent you a goodbye text."

He lifts his head and stares into Pam's eyes with unwavering honesty. "Or someone sent it for her."

"Did you tell the police you suspect it was foul play?"

"Yeah. They brushed me off as a delusional old man."

"Did they dust the gun handle for fingerprints?

"Hell, if I know."

"Do you monitor your house with security cameras?"

"Yeah. One in the front and one in the back."

"What did the video footage show? Did anyone come into your home after you left?"

"I don't know." He shrugs.

"Did you get a notification on your phone?"

"Maybe my wife did. I don't mess with that app bullshit. She bought the camera because of your neighborhood watch meeting."

"I'll help you."

Examining Stan's front porch unit, she could see it is a

'Google Nest Cam', which is more sophisticated than her home system. "Does the video upload to the cloud?"

"What cloud?"

"Never mind. Do you have the username and password?"

"Maybe." Going back into the kitchen, he retrieves a spiral-bound notebook from the drawer.

"She wrote everything down in here. You can use her computer." He motions to the monitor on the desk in the corner of the family room.

Pam turns it on. They both wait patiently for the home screen to load. A desktop photo appears of a much younger Stan, his beaming wife, a stunning woman in a bridal gown, a handsome young man in a tuxedo, and an attractive soldier wearing a dressed-up Army uniform.

"What a beautiful family." Pam is captivated by the picturesque beach scene.

"That's my wife, Debbie, my daughter and son-in-law, and my son in uniform. It was my daughter's wedding day."

Stan sniffs, holding back tears. "It's an old photo."

"Do you mind if I poke around a bit on this computer?"

"Do your thing." Stan pulls up a chair, sitting next to her.

Pam finds the security camera webpage saved in bookmarks, and logs in, using the username and password written in the notebook. Unfamiliar with the layout of the website, she browses for about fifteen minutes.

"Do you know what you're doing?" Stan asks.

"Not really." Pam confesses. "But that's never stopped me before."

After a few minutes of searching, she finds the transaction log. "Oh, my God," she utters quietly to herself.

"What?" Stan perks up.

"The security system was disabled at 10:15 a.m. on the morning your wife was shot."

"It was? Weird."

"I can't figure out how to view the footage. This is a more sophisticated camera than I have. I also don't know how to tell if it was disabled by a cell phone, on the computer, or on the unit itself. Does your wife have an app on her phone?"

"I don't know. Maybe." He goes into the bedroom, returning with her phone. "Damn, the battery is dead."

"I bet she does. Most new systems do." Pam searches further, but is unable to locate the video recording immediately before the unit was turned off. "I'm not familiar with this system, but I find it suspicious that the camera was turned off just when you needed it the most."

"Yeah." Stan scratches his head. "Wait, what are you thinking?"

"Well, when my friend Beth's husband was killed, her security camera messed up the night the incident happened."

"Could there be a connection?"

Pam's eyebrows raise, confirming her light bulb moment. *I need to find out if Richard Johnson's security camera was working the day he died.*

"So nice to meet you, Stan, but I've got to go." Pam stands, "I need to check something. Can I have your phone number?"

Stan tears a page out of the back of the notebook. He jots down his number and hands it to her.

"I'll call you tomorrow." She grabs her purse from the dining room chair and rushes out the door.

On her walk home, Pam stops at Laura Johnson's house to ask her if her security cameras were working the night Richard passed. The 'For Sale' sign now includes an 'Escrow

Pending' banner on the top.

No answer when she knocks on the door. She peeks in the window. The living room is empty and the artwork on the walls has been removed. Inspecting the beams on the front landing, she sees a 'Ring' camera.

The wheels are turning in her head. *I can't tell John I logged into Stan's security system because he'd accuse me of being a busybody, even though Stan gave me the password. Law enforcement is stretched thin. They don't have the time to investigate a death by natural causes, or a suicide. They're barely investigating Marvin Fitzgerald's horrific stabbing!*

CHAPTER FIVE

Pam makes a visit to University of California San Diego to see an old friend. Professor James Leonard teaches information technology. Fifteen years ago, Pam and Steve donated three million dollars to the construction of the building that houses the computer sciences and telecommunications departments. Professor Leonard was ecstatic to have a state-of-the-art facility. He owes her one.

The administrative assistant in the lobby gives Pam directions to the computer lab. She waits in the wide corridor, assuming the class ends on the hour. Professor Leonard exits with his head down, staring at his phone, just like the students.

"Hello, Jim." Pam shouts, as she leans on the window opposite the door.

He glances up at the sound of his name, looking like the stereotypical computer nerd with his slim build, bald head, and black-rimmed glasses, albeit, an old geek.

"Pam? Is that you?" He smiles broadly.

"Yes, it is. A few more pounds of me, but what can I say?" Pam says jovially. "Life's been good."

"You look fantastic." He delivers a tentative hug.

"Can I buy you a cup of coffee?" Pam asks cheerfully.

They go to the campus coffee shop and sit at a table by the window, admiring the architecture of the 'Geisel Library'.

"I have a favor to ask. I have some computer work to do at home. Simple tasks for one of your students, but difficult for me."

"What do you need?"

"I want to verify that my surveillance system is set up correctly, and install a faster WIFI router. I need to bring my house up to date. Stuff like that. I'll pay top dollar. It would only take a couple of hours for someone who's got the skills. I just know enough to make myself dangerous. I'm afraid I'll mess it up."

"I do have a student who is struggling financially, and is about to drop out of school. He's not the top of the class by any means, but he's very bright. I'm sure he could use the money."

"I bet he could help me. I'm willing to pay more than the going rate."

"I'll talk to Peter to see if he wants a side gig."

"Perfect. Please give him my cell number and email address." Pam hands the professor her travel blogger business card.

A week after her coffee klatch with Professor Leonard, she receives an email from Peter. They agree to meet for coffee to discuss Pam's computer needs.

She enters the coffee shop, which is crammed with as many tables as could possible fit in the small space. The aroma of freshly brewed coffee wafts through the air. The place is filled with students glued to their devices. *He could be any one of them.*

Pam orders her latte, then admires the pencil sketches on the wall. Her eyes scan the shop, from the bearded old man in the corner, to a bleach blonde cutie in a low-cut tank top, ignoring the boy's stares. She forgot to ask Peter what color shirt he'd be wearing, or how she could identify him.

"Pam!" Someone shouts her name.

She glances about the shop, trying to determine the source. In the corner, Pam spots a young man with his hand raised as if he's in lecture hall. She approaches him.

"Are you Peter?" She smiles.

"Last time I checked." With his shaggy blonde hair and tanned face, he broadcasts surfer, not computer nerd. He dressed up for the occasion, in his faded blue board shorts, flip-flops, and a white tee shirt. Pam looks like she's attending a job interview, wearing her black pantsuit, multi-colored scarf, and her hair in a chignon.

They chat for fifteen minutes, with Pam explaining the hypothetical tasks needed to be performed at her home. She can turn on the charm, and lie convincingly, when it's warranted by the situation.

"No sweat." Peter says. "What you need is easy peasy."

Pam gains comfort with his level of expertise, so directs the conversation to the real purpose of their meeting.

"Do you remember, about three years ago, there was a news story where a surveillance camera hacker was talking to a young girl in her bedroom through the unit?"

"No, but what a pervert."

"Exactly. It was very scary, but I learned systems can be hacked. Let me cut to the chase." Pam glances over her shoulder. Everyone has their noses buried in their computers, and most of the students are wearing ear buds. "There have been three suspicious deaths recently in my neighborhood. With each one, the security cameras were turned off before the incidents occurred. At least, I suspect so. With one, I believe Mrs. Powalski turned it off herself, but I was unable able to confirm that when I logged into her account. With Marvin

Fitzgerald's murder, there may have been a power outage, and with Mr. Johnson's death, well I haven't researched that yet. That's why I need your help."

"Did you say murder?" An expression of discomfort overcomes his face.

"Yes! And the San Diego Police Department are sitting on their asses. Marvin Fitzgerald and his wife are my friends. Beth won't sleep at night until the criminal who killed her husband is found!"

He leans forward, resting his elbows on the table. "Hacking into security systems must violate some law."

"I'm well aware. I only need you to hack into one system, Richard Johnson's. I have the log in credentials for Stan Powalski, and I can get Beth Fitzgerald's. Can you compile the data for me? I may be able to figure it out, but it would take me hours. And my husband looks over my shoulder when I'm on my laptop. I'd rather avoid having to explain. I know you could do it quicker."

"Sounds like a piece of cake."

"I may be way off base here. If I am, then no one, but you and me, will ever know we hacked in. If my hunch is correct, there is a common thread. I'll go to the police, and they will obtain warrants, or whatever it is they need, to secure the evidence properly. I'm not breaking the law, just bending it a bit."

"Okay, if you say so. Just get me the make, model, and serial number of the system that you don't have the password to. The numbers are usually engraved in very small print on the side of the primary unit. You may need a magnifying glass."

"Once I give you the information, what's next?"

"Just give me a couple days to access the video snippets, and save them on my computer."

"Sounds like a plan. Thanks."

As Pam is driving home, her phone rings. The name 'Stan Powalski' lights up on the infotainment screen of her BMW.

"Hey Stan, what's up?"

"Pam, you're not going to believe this."

"What? What happened?"

"Mr. Ortiz." His voice cracks with distress.

"Who is Mr. Ortiz?"

"He lives next door. Fernando Ortiz."

"What about him?"

"There was a hearse from the mortuary at his house this morning. He died last night."

Death number four in just as many months.

CHAPTER SIX

John painted Beth's guest room and helped her discard some of Marvin's old items. Treasures to Marvin are throwaways to her.

When Pam asked John to paint their dining room a year ago, he shined her on. She had picked out a soothing shade of sage green, which is still sitting in cans in the garage. John is not the people-pleaser type, but he's sure going out of his way for Beth. Pam convinces herself it's okay, giving her more time to write her San Diego visitors blog, and solve the murder mysteries of their neighborhood.

On her morning dog walk, Pam visits Mr. Powalski. She rings the doorbell, listening for the tone. She doesn't hear anything. She then knocks lightly. No answer. She knocks again, practically bruising her knuckles. Hearing shuffling noises, she waits patiently. Stan answers the door, wearing a baggy flannel shirt and faded jeans. His hair is disheveled, and he's rubbing his eyes.

"Did I wake you up?" Pam asks with a cheerful smile.

"No, I got up early." He mumbles.

"Do you have any of that yummy coffee you made last time I was here?"

A grin overcomes his wrinkled face. "You liked it?"

"Yeah." She lies as she steps inside. "Can I put Duke in your backyard?"

"Have at it." Stan goes into the kitchen.

Pam puts her dog in his backyard, then sits at the breakfast table. Stan pours her a mug of terribly strong coffee.

"So sorry to hear about your neighbor." Pam says.

"Yeah, he was a good guy. I was shocked to see the hearse in front of his house."

"What can you tell me about him?"

"Fernando Ortiz was about my age." He wipes a tear off his cheek with this sleeve. "He worked in the yard a lot."

"Do you mind me asking, Stan, how old are you?"

"I'll be seventy-six next week."

"Happy birthday, a week early. So, was Mr. Ortiz sick?"

"If he was, he hid it well. He never talked about aches and pains like old folks do. He was a tough guy, not the kind to want sympathy. He hadn't come out of his house much the last couple of weeks, but a month ago he was mowing the lawn, and washing his pickup truck in the driveway."

"Do you ever talk to his wife?"

"She died about five years ago. I don't remember what was wrong with her. He lived in that big house by himself, and took good care of it. His sons would come over and help him with major projects, like trimming the trees. In fact, Fernando Junior owns a tree trimming business."

"Have you talked to his son?"

"No, not yet." He stands and pulls the curtain back to gaze at the street. "Oh, look at that. Junior's truck is in the driveway."

Pam joins Stan at the window, viewing the vehicle with a cherry picker mounted on the back and a logo stating 'Ortiz Tree Surgery' on the side.

"Let's chat with him." Pam says.

Stan slides on his shoes, checks that his buttons are lined up, and tucks in his shirt.

A few seconds after they knock, a handsome young man with wavy brown hair, and bloodshot eyes, opens the massive wood door. He's wearing jeans, work boots, and a tee shirt with the name of his business across his chest.

"Hello, Mr. Powalski." He stares directly at Stan.

"So sorry, Fernando." Stan expresses kind-heartedly. "I'm going to miss your father. He was a great guy, and a helpful neighbor."

"And an awesome dad." Fernando gazes at the floor, trying to hide his emotions.

"Hello, I'm Pam." Pam offers her hand. He hesitates, then shakes it gently. "We're so sorry for your loss. I live on the next street over." Pam points behind her.

"How did Fernando die?" Stan blurts.

"He died in his sleep." Junior mumbles, as tears stream down his tanned cheeks.

"I guess that's the way to go." Stan replies, then he desperately tries to retract his comment. "I mean, he was too young to die. My heart goes out to your family, I just mean, it sounds like he didn't suffer."

"My sister came over to take him to his doctor's appointment. He was laying in his bed at nine in the morning. She knew something was wrong, because he's always gets up early. She pulled back the covers and he wasn't breathing. He was white as a ghost."

"That's terrible, Fernando," Stan says. "I'm so sorry."

"And I'm sorry about your wife, Mr. Powalski. I just heard about her passing."

"Thank you." Stan utters, choking on his words. A single tear makes a path down his cheek.

"We were shocked by the suddenness of my father's

death, so we requested an autopsy be performed. The coroner was debating if the procedure was necessary because of his age, so he called my dad's doctor. Then the doctor called my sister and told her dad had pancreatic cancer. The coroner said an autopsy wasn't necessary."

"So, it was the cancer that killed him?" Pam asks.

"I guess so. I thought you lasted months, or even years with cancer. I saw him every couple of weeks. He seemed fine the last time I visited."

"I've heard pancreatic cancer is difficult to diagnose early." Pam says caringly. "Can I ask you something?"

He wipes his cheeks with his sleeve. "What?"

"Did your dad have a surveillance system?"

"Yeah, why?" He glances up at the camera tucked away under the overhang of the front landing.

Pam's eyes follow his gaze. *It looks like a 'Ring'.*

She turns to Fernando. "Did you know your father is the fourth death in the neighborhood in the last four months?"

"No, I didn't know that, but mostly old people live around here." He says with a shoulder shrug.

"True, but I just want to verify the deaths aren't related. Do you want to help me?"

He looks at Pam like she's from another planet. "Help you do what?"

"Help me find out if your father's death was cancer, or a murder."

"Murder?" His brows converge in a vee as his glassy brown eyes widen. "Why would anyone want to kill my dad?"

"I hope I'm wrong, but serial killers have no rhyme or reason." Pam defends her claim.

"So, you think a serial killer broke into this house, and killed my dad while he slept?" Fernando snickers. "That's ridiculous."

Stan steps in front of Pam, gently nudging her to the left. "Fernando, I know Pam can come across as a bubble off, but really, she just cares about the safety of the neighborhood. She just wants to make sure nothing fishy is going on. If you just let her do her thing, it will be no harm to you, or your family, and she can satisfy herself that there's not a crazy person running around killing old folks."

"Sounds farfetched, but I guess so." Fernando shrugs.

Pam moves in front of Stan. "The first step would be looking at the footage on the security camera. Do you know if your father received notifications through an app on his phone?"

"Dad was old school. I doubt it."

"Did he have a cell phone?" Stan asks.

"Yes, of course."

"Do you mind if I take a look at it?" Pam asks. "I can tell at a glance if he had the 'Ring" app."

Fernando opens the door wide, motioning for Pam and Stan to come in. I catch a whiff of cigarette smoke as we walk through the terra-cotta tiled foyer into the spacious family room. The well-worn couch, loveseat and recliner are of neutral brown toned fabric. There is a large television perched on a credenza on the opposite wall. Very nineties décor.

"Have a seat." Fernando says.

We sit on the sofa, gazing out the dirty sliding glass door to the overgrown grass in the backyard.

Fernando migrates to a desk in the corner. He shuffles through the papers on top, then rummages through the drawers.

Fernando turns around. "Let me call my sister. She visited more often than me."

He pulls his phone out of his pocket and goes into the kitchen. Pam can faintly hear the conversation.

After a couple minutes, Fernando comes back into the family room. "Okay, got it. Maria said the phone is usually in the charger in the bedroom." He gives us a thumbs up. "She gave me his four-digit log in, and she had recorded his passwords in his notes app. This is why I let my Maria be in charge. She's more organized than me."

He heads to the bedroom. When he returns, he has a phone in hand, and goes to the desk to make notes.

"You can give this a look, but I need my dad's phone. We have stuff we have to close out. So much to deal with."

"I get it." Pam says as he hands her the phone, along with a note where he had scribbled the user name, password, and his phone number. She finds the 'Ring' app, and is able to log in. "Thank you, Fernando. This is great. I'll be able to log in on my laptop at home and do some research."

"Will you let me know if you find anything? My number is on the note."

"Yes, I certainly will." Pam stands, with Stan following her lead. She hands the phone back to Fernando, and stuffs the note in her purse.

"I'll keep everything confidential. I promise. I'm just eager to solve this mystery. Or satisfy myself that these deaths are a non-issue, like my husband keeps telling me."

"Whatever, I don't care." Fernando says. "It won't bring my father back."

John is golfing all day, so he won't be home to look over Pam's shoulder and bug her about being nosey. She logs into the 'Ring' website, with Fernando texting her the security code. She tries to trace the video back to Fernando Senior's date of death, but is unsuccessful.

She calls Peter to tell him there has been a fourth death in the neighborhood. "There is another camera you'll need to check the footage. I've got the log in information, so it will be easy. So, the only system that needs to be hacked is the Johnson's. The house is empty, so I'll get the serial and model number for you. As for the Fitzgerald residence, Beth will give me whatever I ask for."

"Okay Ms. Pam." Peter says. "Call me back with the specifics and I'll get right on it."

Pam grabs her step stool and magnifying glass, and drives to the Johnson residence. She locates the serial number, model number, and manufacturer's name on the unit near the front door. She calls Peter and gives him the information. *Three down, one to go.*

Next stop, Beth's house. Pam's loud knock goes unanswered. The garage door is open, and her Audi, and Marvin's SUV, are in the garage. She gingerly opens the side gate and enters the backyard.

Pam can't believe her eyes. Beth and John are in the pool, sitting on the step, with Beth practically on his lap! Soft rock music is emanating from the wireless speaker. Two stemmed glasses, and a half-filled bottle of wine are on the concrete edge of the pool. Beth giggles as John kisses her on the neck.

Blood wooshes to Pam's cheeks. Her underarm sweats. A combination of anger and disgust simmers within her brain, causing an instant tension headache. She takes two steps back, nearly tripping on the cobblestone. She closes the gate softly.

Jogging back home, she plops into the recliner and tries to compose herself. John cheated on her six years ago with a coworker, before he retired. She gave him a second chance. This time it's her friend! *This is the last straw - no third chance.*

CHAPTER SEVEN

Pam owned her house, and built her fortune, long before she met and married John. *He's not getting a damn dime.* Although she's not capable of physical castration, financial ruin is very doable.

She doesn't say a word to John about his infidelity she witnessed. Business as usual. She smiles when she brings him his coffee, and kisses him goodbye when he leaves to wherever he's going. Her anger has evolved into apathy. She knows lawyers, and just needs to choose one with expertise in divorce proceedings. Then she'll drop the bomb.

After John leaves for the hardware store, Pam brings her laptop into the dining room. She stares out the window and sees Beth's Audi zoom by. *She's on her way to her office downtown.* Pam grabs her step stool and magnifying glass and goes to Beth's house to examine the numbers on the surveillance system. *The blue light is off, so I think the camera is off.*

Pam calls Peter with the details of the Johnson's and Fitzgerald's surveillance cameras. She hopes he can accomplish the video collecting quickly.

Peter calls two days later, interrupting Pam on her daily dog walk. "Miss Pam, I want to show you what I've got."

Pam stops at the corner, allowing Duke the pleasure of sniffing the fire hydrant. "You found something interesting?"

"I think so. Can you come to my apartment and check it out? If it's not what you're looking for, I can dig further."

"Yes, certainly. I'm anxious to solve this mystery, or, if I'm wrong, just drop it. When can I come over?"

"Um…wait a minute." Loud, indiscernible music, and young men's voices are resonating in the background. "I'll be in class most of the day tomorrow. How about three?"

"Three works for me."

The next day she tells John she's going shopping at Neiman Marcus, then heads to Peter's apartment. Pam finds a parking spot on the street and enters the gate of the three-story complex. She ascends the stairs, and wanders the exterior hallways, perusing the numbers on the doors, searching for unit 301. After two knocks, the door opens slowly.

"Who are you?" A petite young man with black rimmed glasses, shaggy brown hair and spotty chin hair looks up at her.

"I'm here to see Peter."

"Peter! Your mom's here!" He yells.

Pam enters warily. "I'm not his mom." She corrects.

The aroma of teenage-boy sweat fills the living room. A guy is sitting on the couch, atop a pile of unfolded blankets, is playing a video game. Another student is sitting in a recliner in the corner, with headphones on, reading a textbook. Another young man is in the kitchen is standing at the stove, slurping ramen. A cute girl with bottle-dyed blue hair, is sitting at the dining table, scrolling her phone.

Peter comes out of the bedroom. "Hey, Miss Pam."

"Hi, Peter. You guys need to open a window in here. How many roommates do you have?"

"Six. This is La Jolla, remember?"

"Oh, yeah."

"My computer is back here." He takes a chair from the kitchen and motions for her to follow him. Pam sits next to him, surveying the small room, seeing a mattress on the floor in two corners.

"Ortiz and Powalski were easy because you gave me the passwords. It took some time, but I was able to hack into Johnson's and Fitzgerald's systems to retrieve footage from the nights you specified."

"I'll pay you for all of your time."

"You certainly will." He smiles. "I don't know what you're trying to prove, but let me show you what I found."

Pulling her pen and notebook out of her purse, she's ready to examine the video. Peter clicks on a folder on the desktop.

"This is the Ortiz house," he says.

Pam stares at the screen closely as the dark video rolls. She spots a woman coming up the walkway to the front landing. She's of stocky build, with a long dark ponytail, swaying back and forth as she walks. It's difficult to see her face because she turns her head away from the camera as she reaches the front door. She's wearing dark jeans, athletic shoes, and a light blue lab coat. The film stops when she reaches the door.

"Can you zoom in any closer? There's a logo on her lab coat." Pam strains to see the embroidery, as Peter zeros in. "I can't make it out."

He expands the view. "A gold star?" She asks.

"Maybe." Peter says. "The next house is Powalski."

He displays the video. The sun is bright, creating a silhouette of a person nearing the entry.

"Look! It's the same woman!" Pam exclaims. "Same height, same ponytail! It's too dark to see her face."

"It might be her, but it's not definitive." Peter replies.

"The lighting is equally terrible in both videos."

"Yeah, but look, it's the same light-blue lab coat." Pam points out, just before the screen goes black.

"What happened?" Pam asked.

"The camera was turned off."

"So, Ortiz and Powalski were the easy ones. What about Johnson. Were you able to hack into their file?"

"Johnson was a 'Ring', so easy to hack." Peter focuses on the monitor, searching for another file. "There were people coming and going, but the camera was never turned off. Not on the date you gave me anyway."

"That blows my theory." Pam exhales a disappointing sigh.

Peter displays the video. Pam views Laura and Richard Johnson coming and going throughout the day. "Can you look at the footage of the day before he died?"

"Sure." Peter reviews his notes, then logs into the 'Ring' website.

They both study the screen attentively.

"There she is!" Pam exclaims. "The stocky woman with a bouncy ponytail and light-blue lab coat. It's her again!"

The quality is better in this video. Pam notices she's wearing minimal makeup, and appears to be in her forties. Her purse is hanging on her shoulder, and she's carrying a soft-sided portfolio bag in one hand, and a drink with a straw in the other. She opens the unlocked door and enters the house.

"Was she carrying a portfolio bag in the other videos?" Pam asks.

"I don't remember. We can check."

"Wait, before you do, back it up. Zero in on her lab coat." Pam instructs. "The logo on it is yellow. It looks like a sun."

"Yeah, sort of." Peter responds.

Next, he locates the video for the Fitzgerald residence. It shows a woman parking in the driveway, and getting out of her car.

"It looks like a late model Mustang." Peters says. "It's red." The screen goes blank.

"Wait, back it up so I can see that again. Can you focus in any closer?"

Pam studies the screen. No ponytail. Her long brown hair is falling in her face, hiding her features. She's wearing a light blue lab coat and dark pants and is about the same size as the woman seen in the other surveillance videos.

"It's got to be the same woman in all four videos!" Pam says. "She must have a connection to the fatalities in the neighborhood."

Peter shrugs his shoulders. "This is your thing."

"What do I do now?"

"Don't ask me." He puts his hands up in arrest mode. "I'm just the computer geek."

Determined to identify the mystery woman, Pam wants to go to the authorities, but can't, because she hacked into the Johnson and Fitzgerald systems illegally. *I don't want to end up in jail myself, but this woman must be stopped!*

CHAPTER EIGHT

The next day, Pam and her labradoodle are on their morning walk. It's a crisp fall day with the misty fog lifting gradually, like a vanishing cloud.

She isn't in the mood to talk to her neighbors, so chooses the bike path that winds through the green belt adjacent to the main road. The oak leaves crunch beneath her feet, as the hum of commuter traffic on La Jolla Boulevard fills her eardrums.

Duke barks for no apparent reason.

"What's up, boy?" She pats his head.

He barks again, then stops in his tracks. "Come on." Pam tugs on the leash. He stretches his retainer to the max, sniffing voraciously under a massive oak tree.

Her dog is laser focused on the dirt, scratching it vigorously. Pam steps off the path, under the canopy of the tree to figure out why Duke is so excited. She squats for keener inspection. The sun shines through the parted fog, highlighting a shiny, half-buried object.

Pam assists Duke in the excavation, being careful not to ruin her manicure. She gingerly loosens the item from the soil.

It's a knife! The wood handle is intricately carved, and

the blade is triangular shaped. Pam's adrenalin skyrockets. *Could this be the dagger missing from Marvin's case?*

Twisting it in her hand, she reveals what appears to be dried blood on the back side of the blade. She extracts a dog poop bag from the pocket of her sweatshirt, and places the knife in the plastic bag. Living with a retired police officer, she's learned the basics of preserving evidence. She can't wait to show the knife to John. He'll know precisely what to do with it.

Racing home, she bursts through the door, gasping for breath. "Look what I found!" Pam yells to John. "This might be the weapon that killed Marvin! Look, look at this!"

He looks up from his iPad. "What did you say?"

Pam shoves the dog into the backyard, then sits by John on the couch. She pulls her find out of the plastic bag.

John stares at the dagger. His cheeks redden as his eyes widen. "Where did you find that?"

"Under an oak tree, by the bike path. Look at the carving on the handle. I bet this is the one missing from Marvin's collection! And look, could this be dried blood? We need to get it to the police for DNA sampling."

She places the weapon judiciously on top of the plastic bag on the coffee table. John hesitates, as he glares at it.

"Slow down, Pam. Maybe this has nothing to do with Marvin's death. That could be a gang symbol on the handle. You need to back off. Those gangsters are smarter than you think. Masters at retaliation."

"There are no gangs around here." She argues.

"Not in this neighborhood, but in San Diego, they're prolific."

She grabs his arm. "Let's go to Beth's and check to see if this is the dagger missing from Marvin's case!"

John waves his hands. "Wait a minute, Pam. I'll make some phone calls. I'll see what I can find out regarding the latest protocols."

John turns back to read his iPad.

"You just said you were going to make phone calls!" Pam stands, with her hand on her hip. "Why are you still sitting there, reading your book?"

He gives her a stern scowl. "Let me think about this."

"What's to think about? I found potential evidence. It needs to be given to the police!"

He focuses on his device, ignoring her load outburst.

"Don't sweat it, John. I wouldn't want you to lift a finger." She glares at him with squinted eyes. "I'll call the police."

Pam goes into the kitchen while John stays in the living room, although she senses he's listening to her every word. She calls the SDPD, asking to speak to the detective handling the Marvin Fitzgerald case.

"Detective Rossi is in a meeting," the receptionist informs Pam. "Would you like to leave a message? He's pretty good about returning his calls."

Pam jots down his name. "Pretty good, huh? Does that mean he will return my call?"

"Yes. I can't tell you exactly when. Most likely, no later than tomorrow." Her voice is precise and her script rehearsed. "What is this regarding?"

"I may have information about the Marvin Fitzgerald stabbing. I found a knife I believe belonged to him."

"Will you hold, please?"

"Sure." Pam waits impatiently, listening to unpleasant elevator music.

"This is Detective Rossi." A deep voice, oozing authority. "How may I help you?"

"I was walking my dog this morning and I found an old knife. I think it has dried blood on it. It looks like it could be from Marvin Fitzgerald's ancient weapons collection. He's my neighbor. And a friend. I should say, was my friend."

"Interesting. Can you bring it to headquarters?"

"Yes, certainly. Right now?"

"I'm finishing up a meeting. After lunch would work out. How about one o'clock?"

"I'll be there at one."

John walks up behind her. "Be where at one?"

"Police headquarters in San Diego, to see Detective Rossi."

"You don't like to listen to me, do you?" He storms out of the kitchen. Pam follows.

"Even if it isn't related to Marvin's murder, and it does belong to a gang banger, I still need to get it to the authorities. How would the gangster even know I was involved?"

"They have their ways." He exits the house to the garage. Pam trails him.

"Where are you going?" She demands.
He jumps in his SUV and slams the door. "What do you care?" His eyes squint in anger.

"You're right." Pam points her index finger at him. "I don't care."

Pam blusters back in the house. *That's it, our marriage is over.* She recounts her multiple reasons for divorcing John, while tensely watching the clock. She needs to leave early enough to allow time for traffic between La Jolla and San Diego.

She places the white plastic bag containing the potential evidence inside a red canvas tote bag, then sets it on the floor in the back seat of her car.

Heading south on the interstate, the radio is blasting nineties rock music. The song transports her back in time, to a happier place in her life when her daughter was a youngster, and her first husband didn't have cancer.

A mile before she reaches the city limits of San Diego, the brake lights of the jacked-up Ford F150 in front of her light up like a drag race Christmas tree. Her right foot slams the brake pedal to the floorboard so hard an intense vibration shoots through her leg to her thigh. The resultant screech, pierces Pam's ears. Skidding below the bumper of the pick-up, the hood of her BMW buckles like an accordion being squeezed. The airbag deploys, slamming Pam forcefully in the chest, thrusting the air out of her lungs. She gasps, sucking in diesel exhaust. Her world turns to darkness.

..

CHAPTER NINE

John receives a call from a highway patrolman notifying him his wife was involved in an accident.

"Is she okay?" he asks, feeling like he just got sucker punched in the gut.

"I don't know the extent of the injuries. She's at UCSD campus medical center," the officer informs in a monotone.

John speeds to the hospital, and enters through the emergency entrance, demanding to see his wife. He's told she's in surgery, and it will be about two hours before he can see her. The nurse is unable to give him details.

While sitting in the waiting room, he's overcome with anxiety. Thoughts race through his mind. The accident happened when Pam was delivering the bloody weapon to the detective. *What if she was a target?*

Every fifteen minutes, he bugs the receptionist for the status of his wife. He's lost track of time, but guesses at least two hours have passed. Finally, a nurse comes into the waiting room asking for Mr. Guerrero.

"I'm here." John raises his hand.

"Mr. Guerrero, your wife is in the recovery room. When I'm told her room number, I'll inform you."

"Where is the doctor? Why hasn't he come out to tell me what's going on?"

"You'll have to be patient," she says with a faux smile.

Grabbing a 'Golf Digest' magazine, he thumbs through it nervously, perusing the photos, while his leg jitters. Sweat trickles down his temples. He's worried about Pam, yet also pissed off at her. She doesn't listen to him anymore, and retreats into her own travel blogging, crime solving world. *She drove me into Beth's arms.* Their marriage, which began on an emotionally rebounded foundation, has deteriorated into an empty shell of tolerance. They both realize it, but refuse to admit it to themselves, and each other.

Finally, the nurse gives him the room number and directions to the fourth floor.

John's eyes water as he traverses the sterile corridor, checking the numbers posted outside each room. He gets a whiff of strong disinfectant as he locates Pam's room. He takes a deep breath before he carefully opens the door.

His wife is lying in bed, lifeless, drained of color, with a gauze bandage plastered across her cheek. The whooshing sound of the ventilator is eerily rhythmical, like there's a ghost behind him, breathing down his neck. Pam's arms is hooked to an IV. Her legs are covered by a cotton blanket. He feels his knees weaken as his eyes flood with tears of guilt.

A petite woman in a white lab coat with short black hair, holding a clipboard, enters the room. "Who are you?" she asks bluntly.

"I'm her husband. Who are you?" His tone is equally insolent.

"I'm Doctor Sima. Her foot was fractured in two places, and she ruptured her spleen. The impact was traumatic. We set her foot, and repaired her spleen."

"Why does she have a bandage on her check?" John

asks with watery eyes.

"She has an abrasion. But it's not deep."

John exhales a stress relieving breath. "Will my wife be okay?"

"She's fortunate. It could have been much worse. She'll recover from her injuries."

"That's good news." John sighs. "How long will it take?"

"She will need physical therapy because her foot has multiple fractures. I would estimate in about eight weeks she could start therapy. We need to give it time to heal. The spleen will take a few months longer, but that shouldn't cause her any pain. She'll definitely need to take it easy for a while. What is her level of activity?"

"Walking is her primary source of exercise, so this will be a significant adjustment."

"In a few weeks, she can use crutches. It will help to rebuild bone. The nurse will give you instructions for taking care of her. She will need to be on pain meds the first week or two."

John stays by her bedside, waiting for her to wake up. Another hour passes. He's beyond fatigued, so goes to the cafeteria for a cup of coffee. When he returns, Pam's eyes are open. He tenderly lifts her hand into his. She turns her head.

"John," she utters.

"Pam, I'm here. What happened?"

"I was on the freeway. The truck in front of me slammed on their brakes."

"Unbelievable." He rubs his bloodshot eyes.

"It wasn't my fault."

"I know." John reassures her. He stays by her side until she falls asleep for the night.

The next morning, he wakes up in a cold, empty bed,

with his heart feeling just as vacant. *This has gotten too complicated.*

He calls the wrecking yards, and locates Pam's BMW on the second try. He's informed by the dispatcher that her vehicle is sitting on the back of the truck.

"Is it totaled?"

"Definitely. The front end is smashed big time." The wrecking yard employee replies.

"I'm her husband. When can I retrieve my wife's personal items from her car?"

"In about an hour, I guess."

John shows up promptly in an hour to clean out the contents of Pam's vehicle. He empties the glove box of the registration, sunglasses, breath mints and pens, and tosses them into the red tote bag he finds in the back seat. Then he piles the junk in the center console on top of it. Opening the trunk, he finds the battery charger, reusable grocery bags, and a blanket.

He calls the San Diego Highway Patrol Headquarters and requests they email the incident report to him as soon as it's available. Based on the officer's detailed verbal description, he extrapolates that the accident was likely Pam's fault. In less she can prove that the driver of the pick-up slammed on his brakes for no apparent reason. He fears there's a lawsuit in their future.

After four nights in the hospital, Pam is released, provided she secures around the clock care. John is up to the challenge. He took care of his first wife in her last days, so is an experienced caregiver, albeit a reluctant one.

Renting a hospital bed and buying a new smart television, he gets the downstairs guest room set up for his wife's convalescence.

A week dawdles by. Pam is frustrated that she's still on prescription narcotics. She wants to get back on her computer, and learn how to use crutches.

John does an excellent job coordinating her medications, cooking, and cleaning, but they aren't used to being together twenty-four seven. They both need a break from each other. Pam can sense he's antsy, like a caged animal.

"If you want to shoot a round of golf today, John, I'll be fine. Thank you for taking such good care of me. With the remote, and my laptop, I can entertain myself."

"Great idea, but are you sure?"

"Yes, I'll be okay."

"I am going a little stir crazy." He hands her the remote.

"I won't be too late." John delivers a forced kiss on Pam's cheek, and leaves.

She switches the channel to news, then scans her email and social media accounts for correspondence she missed while incapacitated. She can't wait until the fuzziness in her brain subsides so she can get back to writing her travel blog.

Checking her calendar, she notices John is scheduled to play in a golf tournament in Santa Barbara in a week and a half.

Pam's phone on the nightstand vibrates. Beth's name illuminates. She hesitates, unsure if she wants to talk to the slut whose banging her husband. She picks up her phone, noticing a missed call from a number she doesn't recognize.

"Hello, Beth." Pam forces herself to sound cheerful.

"Oh, Pam, John told me about the accident. I'm so worried about you. How are you?"

"I'm doing better each day. John's been waiting on me hand and foot."

"Can I come over? I have been wanting to visit, but I didn't want to interrupt."

I don't even want to talk to this two-faced bitch, let alone, see her.
"That would be fine." Pam lies. "The front door is locked, so just come through the gate into the backyard. The door into the garage is unlocked."

Twenty minutes later Beth calls out as she enters the kitchen. "Pam? Where are you?"

"In the guest room!" Pam shouts. "No stairs for me."

Beth is holding a bouquet of multi-colored roses. "I picked these for you from my yard."

Pam sits up in bed. "Those are beautiful. Thank you."

Beth leans over and gives her a reticent hug. "Oh, my dear, what happened?"

"Just driving on the freeway. The pickup in front of me slammed on their brakes. I broke my foot in two places. I'll be able to start using crutches soon."

Beth puts the flowers in a vase and makes a cup of coffee for both of them. They catch up on what their children and grandchildren have been doing.

"How are things with your business?" Pam asks.

"Very busy. I've recently hired four more caregivers. It's time-consuming checking references and doing background checks, but it's got to be done."

"It's good to keep busy."

"I agree, but at my age, I need to slow down a bit. Marvin often told me not to work so much, but I didn't listen to him."

Pam refrains from telling Beth she found a weapon that could be the one missing from Marvin's case. Ever since she saw her frolicking in the pool with John, she doesn't trust her. The status of the knife is for law enforcement to decide. *The knife!* Pam remembers that delivering it to the detective was the purpose of her trip when the accident occurred. *What happened to it?* She has calls to make; the wrecking yard, Detective Rossi, her daughter in Texas, and Stan Powalski. And she needs to check her messages.

"Thanks for coming over." Pam interrupts Beth's blabbing about a fender bender she experienced years ago. "I'm getting tired. I need a nap."

"Of course." She pats Pam's arm lovingly. "You need your rest. Let me know how I can help. I bet John's been taking good care of you, but maybe he needs a break."

"He's on a break right now." Pam snaps at Beth with suspicion, knowing her so-called friend is more concerned with John's well-being than her own. "He's golfing."

"Okay, then." She stands and smooths the slight wrinkles of her tailored emerald green dress. "I'll see you later. Hope you feel better soon." She lets herself out.

Pam grabs her phone. Detective Rossi left a message the day after the accident, asking why she had missed her appointment.

She immediately calls John, interrupting his game. "John, did you take the knife to Detective Rossi?"

"What knife?"

"The knife I found the morning of the accident. You know, when I was walking Duke."

"What are you talking about?" Muffled voices of his golf buddies create indiscernible chatter in the background.

"It needs to be delivered to Detective Rossi."

"Who?" John asks with a laugh. He's listening to his friends, not her.

"The detective handling Marvin's case!" She shouts into the phone.

"There was no knife in the car. Is that where you were going when you got in the accident?"

"Yes, I told you that."

"No, you didn't." John says flippantly.

"Detective Rossi needs it. It was in a plastic bag, inside a red canvas tote bag on the floor in the backseat. Where is it?"

"I just told you. There was no knife in the car."

Pam hangs up on him, then searches for wrecking yards

on her iPad, and calls the correct one on the first try. The manager tells her the vehicle was totaled, and her husband cleared out the contents the same day the tow truck delivered her BMW to the lot. *Either someone stole the knife from the back seat, or John is lying.*

CHAPTER TEN

Pam's current state of dependency depresses her. She's hobbling on crutches, requiring pain medication, and can't stand the fogginess permeating her brain.

She sits at the breakfast nook while John searches the freezer for something to cook for dinner.

"We need to talk about this weekend." Pam says. "I want you to go Santa Barbara, really, I do, I'm just not sure if I'm up to a long weekend alone. I'll call Jill to come out. We can pay her airfare."

"Too short of notice for her." He shakes his head. "A lot of hassle for just two nights."

"We haven't seen her since the summer. I would love to see her and the kids again. It would lift my spirits."

"I have an idea." He sits in the chair next to her. "We hire a caregiver from 'Sunset Health' while I'm gone."

"I guess that could be an option."

"The best option. Call Beth. She'll arrange for someone to watch after you. You know she'll give us a huge discount. That would be easier."

"You might be right." Pam grudgingly agrees.

After dinner, Pam gives Beth a call. She answers after one ring.

"How is your foot, Dear?" Beth sounds sincerely concerned.

"I'm doing okay. I need to talk to you about this weekend. John is out of town, and I need some caretaking. You're the expert."

"I'd hang out with you myself, but I'll be out of town." *Yeah, likely in Santa Barbara humping my husband.*

"Just tell me what you need," Beth adds, "and I'll arrange it."

"Basically, I just need someone to check on me in the evening. John's afraid I'm going to take a fall since I'm uncoordinated on these crutches. All this sitting, I'm sure my ass is getting wider by the minute. If a caregiver could cook dinner, that'd be extremely helpful."

"You've got it, Pam. And you'll receive the friends and family discount."

On Friday John is up as the sun rises, packing his suitcase.

"Are you sure you'll be okay?" John asks, as he zips his suitcase closed.

"I'll be fine. You go have a wonderful time." Pam says, faking sincerity. "The weather will be ideal for golf."

"I'll be home Sunday evening, about five."

Pam is waiting for him to say those three words. He doesn't, because it would be a lie. She doesn't love him anymore either. Sometimes she supposes she does, like these last few weeks when he's been taking care of her, but his attentiveness is temporary. He's having a lurid affair with Beth. When the timing is right, she's leaving him. She needs to build her health back first.

Settling into the bed with all she needs in reach; the

remote, her phone, her laptop, and coffee, she's ready for methodical binge watching. She catches up on 'Downtown Abbey', while intermittently working on her blog.

Pam remembers she needs to call Stan Powalski to tell him about the discovery of the mystery woman on the surveillance footage.

"Hello, Stan, how are you?"

"Okay, I guess. How are you?"

"Well, not well. I rammed into the back of a pick-up a couple of weeks ago. I broke my foot and ruptured my spleen."

"What? Are you kidding me?"

"I'm not. I'm getting around a little now. We need to talk. Can you come over?"

"I guess so."

"The front door is locked. Go into the backyard, then into the garage, and through the kitchen." Pam reiterates her address to Stan. He arrives thirty minutes later.

"How did this happen?"

"The truck I was tailgating slammed on its brakes. It happened so fast."

"How screwed up is that? Are you in pain?"

"I was at first, not so much now. Well, pain killers help."

"Drugs are a beautiful thing." He gazes at the wall, as though he is reminiscing about his younger days.

"I have to tell you what the computer hacker found." Pam says, zapping him out of his daydream.

"If you say so." He sits in the chair, elbows on his knees, leaning forward to be sure he can hear Pam.

"There is a mystery woman showing up in each of the videos. At your house, the camera was turned off as she entered the front door."

"Really? Maybe she was the one who pulled the trigger."

He says facetiously.

"At Fernando Ortiz's house, same thing. The mystery woman turned off the camera as she entered. At Richard Johnson's, the same woman entered, although she didn't turn off the camera. And with Beth, her power was out."

"Okay." Stan pauses. "It sounds like you don't have anything definitive."

"Well, we do need more information."

"We? It's the police who need more information." He shakes his head. "Pam, I have my doubts you know what you're doing."

"We need more information, but let me tell you the rest of the story." Pam says excitedly. "The morning of my accident, I found a bloody knife when I was on my walk. I think it was the dagger used to kill Marvin Fitzgerald."

"What did the police say?"

"They haven't seen it yet! I was on my way to police headquarters when I rammed into the back of a truck. John took it out of the back seat of my car. I know he did."

"Why would he not take it to the detective for you?"

"He thinks it belongs to a gang banger, and if they found out I submitted the evidence, my life is in danger."

"That sounds a little farfetched."

"He's a retired cop. And a pessimist."

"Where is he now?" He glances toward the kitchen, anticipating that John will walk in any second.

"Santa Barbara, on a golf weekend. I need your help. You've got to find the knife! I'm too disabled at the moment. Knowing John, it's hidden somewhere in the garage. I stay out of his domain. Search the cabinets, the tool box, all that." She clutches his arm in desperation. "I need you to find it, Stan."

"What am I looking for, exactly?"

"A red canvas tote bag, with a white plastic bag inside.

Or just a white plastic bag. In less John repackaged it, or, if someone stole it from the backseat of my car."

"Stole it from your car?"

"Never mind. John found it; I know he did. Just look in every bag or container you can. I've got to find it!"

"I'll give it a try." Stan shrugs his shoulders.

He makes his way through the kitchen into the garage. The left wall is plastered with hefty hooks holding various tools and landscaping equipment. The opposite wall has cabinets, a work bench and a two freestanding tool boxes. After fumbling to find the light switch, he starts with the cabinets. One by one he rummages through each one; spray paint, nails, screws, glues, staple gun, tie downs, bungee cords, you name it John has got it.

After an hour of exploration, Stan comes in the house for a drink.

Pam is propped up in bed scrolling the channels. The door slams as Stan enters. "Did you find it!" She yells.

Stan shuffles into the bedroom. "I need something to drink."

"I have bottles of iced tea in the fridge. And sparkling water."

"Got anything stronger?" He asks with a grin.

"You have a job to do." She scolds.

"You owe me one." He heads to the kitchen, grabs a sparkling water, and returns to the garage. Searching behind the tool box, he then goes through them drawer, by drawer. In the bottom section of the second box, he spots something white below a pile of wrenches and pliers. Stan gingerly removes the wrenches, as though they're breakable. He unburies the white plastic bag. Opening the bag, he peers inside, seeing a long-bladed knife with an intricately carved handle.

He rushes into the house. "Is this it?" He asks, as he

hands the bag to Pam.

She yanks it from him and opens it wide "Yes! You found it. Where was it?"

"It was buried in the bottom drawer of the toolbox with small hand tools piled on top of it."

"I knew John found it!"

"Imagine that. It was in the last place I looked." Stan puffs his chest with pride.

She smiles. "I knew John lied to me. Thank you so much, Stan. I knew it was in the garage somewhere."

"If your husband wanted it to disappear, why didn't he just throw it in a dumpster?"

Pam hesitates, focusing on Stan's question. "Wait, I know why. This dagger is worth a lot of money. It was part of Marvin's medieval weapons collection."

She grabs her computer and begins googling *Cinquedea*, a name forever ingrained in her memory. She finds a similar dagger listed for sale on a London auction house website.

"This knife is worth about forty thousand dollars! That's why John couldn't toss it."

"Wow, that's a lot of dough."

"Um, John helps me with my clothes, so I can't hide it in the closet. It must be somewhere he would never look. Stan, can you put it in my laptop bag? That navy-blue canvas bag over there." Pam points under the desk.

Stan complies, then glances at his watch. "I better go."

"You got an appointment?" Pam inquires, knowing he doesn't.

"No." He shrugs his soldiers. "Not really."

The alarm on Pam's phone rings, reminding her that a caregiver from 'Sunset Health' will arrive in ten minutes.

"Wait, Stan. If you could just help me out of bed, I can go to the bathroom by myself." Pam slides her legs to the side of the bed and grabs her crutches leaning on the chair.

"Glad to know you can crap on your own." He flashes an embarrassed grin.

She hobbles to the bathroom, and tells him to listen for the doorbell.

Pam returns to bed and rearranges the pillows to get comfortable, while Stan sits in the chair next to the bed, flipping channels.

They glance at each other when they hear the doorbell.

"I'll get it." Stan volunteers. He greets the woman at the door.

"Hello, I'm Olivia Jones." She flashes a friendly grin, showing crooked teeth. Her captivating brown eyes are highlighted by thick eyeliner and drawn on eyebrows. She's got a couple of inches, and a few pounds on him.

"I'm Stan. Pam is in the guest room." He points to the downstairs bedroom.

"Thanks." She passes through the family room, down the short hall to the room.

"Hello, Mrs. Pam Guerrero," she says cheerfully. "I'm Olivia Jones from 'Sunset Health'."

Pam's throat closes. Her eyes widen in disbelief. *Oh, my God. It's her! She's in my house! In my room!* Olivia Jones; a stocky built woman with long brown hair pulled in a high ponytail, wearing dark jeans, and a light blue lab coat with a yellow 'Sunset Health' logo on the left side of her chest. Her purse is hanging from one shoulder, and a black leather satchel from the other.

Olivia extends her hand. "Pleasure to meet you." She delivers precise eye contact. Her hand is clammy with sweat. Pam perceives the hollowness of her soul in her malevolent brown eyes. She's thinking that this caregiver is likely the last face her neighbors' saw before crossing over to the other side.

I'm not ready for the other side.

"Um, happy to meet you, Olivia." Pam stutters. "Thanks for coming."

"I'm out of here." Stan says casually.

"No! You can't." Pam shouts.

He raises his brows in confusion. Pam glares at him, as she inhales deeply, gaining her composure. Then she turns to Olivia.

"This is my neighbor, Stan. We were just about to have a confidential conversation. Do you mind?"

Olivia glances at Stan. Then back at Pam. "No problem. I'll be in the kitchen, looking through your refrigerator. I'm cooking dinner for you tonight." She smiles broadly. "You relax, Miss Pam. I'm here to get you anything you need."

Pam motions for Stan to close the bedroom door after Olivia exits.

"That's her." Pam whispers.

"Who?"

"The woman in the videos."

"What videos?"

"The ones I told you about earlier that Peter compiled for me. This is the same home health care worker who went to your house right before your wife was shot! And Richard Johnson's. And Fernando Ortiz's. And Marvin Fitzgerald's."

"Are you sure?" Stan matches her hushed tone. "She seems so nice."

"Did you notice what kind of car she was driving?"

He goes to the window and pulls back the drapes.

"There's a shiny red Mustang in your driveway. Um, awesome car."

"That's her. The mystery woman drives a Mustang. You can't leave me alone with her! She might try to kill me."

"Maybe you're wrong, Pam. I mean, could you be

overreacting?"

"I hope I am, but I mean it, Stan," Pam seizes his arm, "you must stay here."

"I guess I could. And have dinner with you?"

"I'm not eating whatever food that murderer makes, but, yes, you need to stay until she leaves. Now, open the door so she doesn't think we're talking about her."

"But that's exactly what we're doing."

"Just open the door."

Olivia comes back in the bedroom and questions Pam about the details of her accident, feigning a sympathetic ear. Stan crosses his legs, looking uncomfortable in the chair, sensing his presence is creating an awkward threesome.

"Will you be staying for dinner, Mr. Stan?" Olivia's tone is overly polite.

He turns to Pam, as if she needs to answer for him.

"Yes." Pam blurts. "Although I'm not very hungry. The last thing I need is extra calories."

"I saw chicken in your meat drawer. How about a grilled breast and a salad?"

"That will be plenty."

Olivia retreats to the kitchen. They hear the clamoring of cupboards opening and closing.

"Stan, you need to look in her black portfolio bag."

"Why?"

"She's stashing poison in there. Or drugs. Or a weapon. I can feel it. This is the woman who put the gun in your wife's hand and pulled the trigger. We could be next."

CHAPTER ELEVEN

Pam and Stan stay in the guest room, watching the news, while Olivia is cooking.

"We can act like we're eating," Pam instructs, "but we'll wrap our food up in a napkin and throw it in the trash. I don't want to risk her poisoning me."

"The pain meds are getting to you." Stan shakes his head. "Why would this woman want to kill you?"

"She's a serial killer." Pam whispers. "A psychopath. They don't need a reason. They're irrational. I'm going to tell Beth about her murderer employee, but I need more evidence before making such a serious accusation."

Twenty minutes later, Olivia enters the bedroom and places a plate of food on Pam's rotating hospital table. The dish contains an appetizing golden-brown chicken breast with green beans and a small spring mix salad squeezed on the side.

"I made a meal for you too, Mr. Stan. Pam, do you have a TV tray?"

"Yes, it's in the closet near the foyer, by the vacuum cleaner."

Stan jumps up to get the portable table, while Olivia retrieves his plate.

"Looks delicious." Stan shoves his napkin into the top of his shirt like a toddler's bib. He cuts the meat, and pops a bite into his mouth. Pam glares at him.

"I'm going to clean the mess in the kitchen," Olivia announces. "please let me know if you need anything else."

"We're fine." Pam says. "Thank you, Olivia."

After Olivia is out of earshot, Pam scolds Stan. "You're actually eating that? Why?"

"I'm hungry. It's been a while since I've had a home cooked meal." He eats a huge bite of chicken.

"It could be poisoned."

"You're paranoid, Pam. And at this point in my life, I don't care." He scarfs the green beans.

Pam moves the food around on the plate with her fork, then shuffles it into her napkin, making it appear as though she consumed most of her meal.

"Stan, when Olivia goes to the bathroom, I need you to look inside her bag."

"What do you want me to look for?"

"A gun, a knife, poison, drugs, whatever."

"I'll try, but what you're asking may not be possible."

Stan tosses Pam's napkin full of uneaten food into the trash can by the bed. Then he wanders into the kitchen with their dirty plates. Olivia is washing the grill pan as she gazes out the window to the street. He spots her black leather satchel sitting on a chair at the breakfast nook.

"Thanks for the dinner. It was good."

"You're very welcome." She says, with a friendly smile.

"Is that your Mustang out there?"

"Yes, that's my wheels." Olivia states proudly.

"Nice car."

"I love it. I've wanted a Mustang for years, and finally bought one about a year ago."

"How long have you been caretaking?"

"About five years. Two for 'Sunset Health'."

"Seems like a difficult job."

"It really is my calling. I enjoy taking care of others."

Stan's contemplating how he could distract her, so he could look in her black bag. Pam said to do it when she goes to the bathroom. That hasn't happened yet. With no clear plan to distract Olivia, he heads back into the bedroom to chat with Pam.

Before he has a chance to speak, Pam blurts "I just heard her go to the bathroom." She points in the direction of the downstairs half-bath, prompting him to perform the task she recommended.

He turns around and gazes back to the kitchen. "I don't have enough time."

"Yes, you do." Pam insists.

A few seconds later Olivia exits the bathroom, humming an indiscernible tune as she heads into the kitchen.

"See, I told you so. She's too fast." Stan shrugs his shoulders. "I have an idea, I'll let the air out of her tire. When she's changing it, I'll look in her bag."

"Bad idea. She'll ask you to change it for her."

"She weighs more than I do. Look at her. She's sturdy. She's probably changed more tires in her lifetime than you and me put together."

Fiddling with his wiry gray beard, Stan is deep in thought. He stands and grins at Pam mischievously, as he pulls his flip phone out of his pants pocket. "I'm going outside to make a call."

Pam bows her head, fearing what he has in mind.

Stan struts out of the house, past the front yard, and into the street, with his phone to his ear. About five minutes later he comes back into the guest room.

"I need to borrow your phone," he splays his hand open.

"Why?"

"Mine doesn't have a camera."

Pam reluctantly points to her phone sitting on the end table.

"What's your passcode?" Stan asks.

Pam whispers her four-digit number. "Do you know how to take a photo?"

"Yeah, my wife had an iPhone. Aren't they all the same?" He examines Pam's phone, inadvertently snapping an image of his shoe.

"Yeah, pretty much." Pam responds. "What are you taking pictures of?"

"You'll see." He slides her phone in his shirt pocket then goes into the kitchen to chat with Olivia.

"What are you making?" He clicks his nails on the kitchen counter in a nervous, rhythmic pattern.

"I found a box of brownie mix. Doesn't that sound tasty?"

"Yeah, it does." Leaning on the counter, he folds his arms across his chest, watching her every move.

She gets an egg from the refrigerator, cracks it into the batter, and begins stirring vigorously.

Suddenly, a loud crash, like a brick was thrown through the dining room window, startles them. Olivia drops the spoon in the bowl and rushes to the kitchen window.

"What the hell!" she exclaims. "Some punk just bashed the rear window of my Mustang with a baseball bat!" She rushes out the front door and chases the hoodlum down the street.

Now's my chance. Grabbing her leather satchel from the chair, Stan zips it open. On the right side are boxes of gauze, band-aids, a bottle of hydrogen peroxide strapped in its place, and white tape. On the left side are plastic wrapped needles, face masks, and numerous vials of liquid with very small print.

He quickly snaps photos of the items, zeroing in on the vials. He reaches in the pockets and finds more amber colored prescription drug bottles and vials. He snaps a photo of each of them, being careful to replace them in the correct slot.

Stan hears the creak of the front door opening. Olivia is panting like a dog. He frantically zips the bag closed. He tries to remember exactly how it was set on the chair. *I hope this is right.* Olivia enters the kitchen, out of breath and bearing an angry scowl.

"God damn that punk!" She gasps for air. "I chased him halfway down the block, but he's too fast. God dammit, what an asshole!" She pauses and glares at Stan. Her eyes are flaming with anger. "I know who did this."

"You...um...do?" Blood rushes to his cheeks, turning them beet red.

"My damn brother-in-law."

The tension filled breath Stan was holding whooshes from his mouth, as his shoulders slump. "Family drama?"

"I can't even go there." She flings the brownie batter into a pan, shoves the baking pan into the oven, then begins washing the bowl.

Stan slips back into the bedroom to check on Pam. "What happened?" She whispers. "What was that crash I heard?"

"She thinks her brother-in-law hired the punk."

"What are you talking about? Why are you smiling?"

He places Pam's phone in her hand. "Tell you later." The plodding of Olivia's feet behind him echoes in his ear. "Look at the photos after she's gone." He whispers.

Pam puts it on the end table, screen side down. Olivia comes in announcing that brownies will be ready soon. She doesn't say a word about the damage to her car. Stan and Pam resume watching 'Jeopardy' as if nothing happened.

Thirty minutes later, Oliva presents a plate of warm brownies, fresh out of the oven. Even though Pam is starving, she passes on the treats with the excuse she's counting calories. Stan possesses no fear of getting poisoned, so eats three of them.

"These are delicious," he mumbles with his mouth full.

"Glad you like them." Olivia responds with a smile. She turns to Pam. "Do you need help changing into your pajamas?"

"No thank you. I can sleep in these sweats."

"Are you sure? Are you comfortable?"

"Yes, I'll be fine."

"Okay, I'll see you tomorrow. Same time."

They listen for the closing of the front door, and the roar of Olivia's Mustang.

Stan explains to Pam that he called his grand-nephew to come and beat the hell out of Olivia's rear window with a baseball bat. "My nephew will do anything for money."

"So, what was the point?"

"To distract her long enough for me to take photos of the contents of her bag."

They scroll through the photos on Pam's iPad, expanding them to view the fine print. They find valium, pentobarbital, secobarbital, sodium phenobarbital, and ofloxacin. Pam googles the drug names. They're mostly sedatives.

"These could kill someone." Pam says.

"Well, that depends on the dose." Stan says. "Even booze is lethal if you drink too much at one time."

"I know, but why would she need such a variety of powerful drugs?"

"Maybe it's normal for caregivers to have that stuff."

"I don't think it's normal. If you would have seen those videos, her going to the houses of everyone who died, you'd be thinking the same as me."

"Pam, you're overreacting."

"No, I'm not."

"Are you going to be okay here alone? I mean, if the house caught fire or something, you couldn't even get out in time with your lame foot."

"What a reassuring thought." Pam huffs as she snuggles deeper under the covers. "I'll be fine. Just lock the front door on your way out."

.

CHAPTER TWELVE

The next morning Pam rolls herself into the bathroom on her wheeled office chair. She had a good night's sleep. For the first time in weeks, she doesn't wake up with a headache. Her mind is abundantly clear.

So glad I'm done with those pain killers. Maybe Stan is right. Maybe I'm overreacting. Maybe Olivia isn't a serial killer. Beth screens her employees thoroughly.

Instead of making Stan babysit her again tonight, Pam has a plan.

When she bought more 'Blink' cameras, after Marvin's murder, she ended up with two extras lying around. She hobbles to the closet to retrieve the box and sets one on the small table in the guest room, below the television. Relocating a potted fern from the living room, she places it halfway in front of the small black device. It is nearly hidden. She checks the view on her phone. After a few adjustments, it's aimed perfectly at the bed.

Pam sets up the other unit discreetly on a knick-knack shelf in the kitchen, wedged between antique spice cans. Checking the view on her iPad app, she makes the appropriate tweaks. *Perfect.* Now she can see the breakfast nook, and the stove against the opposite wall.

With the two 'Blink' devices Pam can watch her caregiver's every move.

The day drags. Pam is so sick of TV and reading political Instagram posts. She might have to call Stan to come over to alleviate her boredom. Even though John is a cheating, argumentative jerk, he does provide companionship.

Pam's about to doze off, when the alarm on her phone wakes her up. Time for Olivia's arrival.

She catches Olivia's raspy voice as she calls out upon entering the house. "Oh, Miss Pam, I'm here."

Olivia enters the bedroom with a purse on one shoulder, and her black, soft-sided satchel on the other. She's wearing her usual attire; black jeans, a yellow polo shirt and a light blue 'Sunset Health' lab coat. Her thick brown hair is styled in a braid to the side, dangling over her right breast.

"How are you feeling today?"

"Quite well." Pam absorbs her congenial expression. *How could someone so polite be a cold-blooded killer?* Her pupils aren't wicked like they were yesterday.

"Each day I feel a little better. My mind is clearer."

"Wonderful." Olivia says supportively. "What would you like for dinner?"

"I'm not very hungry. And my husband hasn't gone shopping in a week."

"I'll figure something out." She goes into the kitchen.

Through the 'Blink' app on her iPad, Pam spots Olivia placing her purse on one of the breakfast table chairs, and her black bag on another. She checks her phone, then she rummages through the freezer, pulling out a frozen package and moves back to the pantry, retrieving a packet of corn tortillas.

Olivia enters the bedroom. "How about fish tacos?"

Pam holds her iPad close to her chest, hiding the

screen. "Love them. But when I make them, they're barely edible."

"Tacos it is. I guarantee you will like them. Will your friend, Stan, be joining you?"

"No." Pam shakes her head.

Pam contemplates if she will eat the potentially poisoned food. *Fish tacos do sound delicious.*

Pam views her iPad again, and opens the 'Blink' app. She sees Olivia in profile as she fills the sink with water, places the fish package in the bath, then peruses the spice rack. Pam keenly scrutinizes her every move, trying to catch her extracting a poisonous additive from her bag and adding it to Pam's meal.

Olivia begins cooking the fish in olive oil in a high sided sauté pan, then chops lettuce and avocado. Seeing her create the dish is whetting Pam's appetite. She doesn't notice anything awry in the cooking method. Olivia turns off the stove and heads to the bedroom.

Pam slams the cover of her iPad closed, and focuses on the news broadcast blasting from the television.

"Miss Pam, what would you like to drink with your meal?"

"Iced tea with two teaspoons of sugar please."
"You got it." Olivia grins and mimics a gun point of her index finger.

She returns to the bedroom ten minutes later with a dish of two grilled fish tacos topped with lettuce, grated cheese and avocado, artfully arranged on the plate with orange slices on the side.

"I couldn't find any tomato."

"This looks yummy. No tomato needed." Pam didn't see Olivia add anything to the food, so she'll take her chances.

As Pam munches on her tacos, she keeps a keen eye on Olivia washing the pan and placing it in the lower cupboard.

Next, Olivia takes a Modelo from the refrigerator, opens it, and guzzles half the bottle. She pulls her shoulders back and rolls her head like an athlete warming up for a sporting event.

Pam watches Olivia closely on her iPad. She sees her zip open her black portfolio bag. She pulls out a vial and a hypodermic needle. Using a syringe, she carefully extracts the liquid from a vial and transfers it to the chamber of the needle, flicking it twice with her finger. She places the needle in the right pocket of her lab coat, then repeats the process, placing the second needle in her left pocket.

Are those intended for me. She grabs her iPhone from the nightstand and touches Stan's number.

"Stan, I need you to come over."

"What? Why?" He sounds like he just woke up.

"She's going to kill me." Pam whispers in the phone.

"What? Who?"

"Olivia. She's following up on last night. She's going to finish me off. Finish the job she came to do. You need to come over here, NOW. With my broken foot, I won't be able to fight her off!'"

"She's going to beat you up?"

"Just get your ass over here."

"On my way." Click.

Stan slips on his shoes, and jacket, and jumps in his pick up truck.

CHAPTER THIRTEEN

Stan twists the knob of the front door. It's locked. *Pam might be in danger. Stealth entry is required.* He goes to the side gate and quietly lets himself into the yard, then enters through the side door into the garage.

Entering the kitchen, he startles Olivia, finding her finishing off a bottle of beer. Her hair is pulled back in a low pony tail, revealing a weird neck tattoo.

"Crap! Don't sneak up on me like that!" She shouts. The angry eyes Stan noticed yesterday have returned.

Pam overhears Olivia's outburst. A sense of assurance comes over her, knowing Stan has arrived.

"Hello, Olivia." Stan bellows.

"What are you doing here? I mean, Pam said you weren't coming over. You missed dinner."

"I ate already. So, it appears I'm here in time for happy hour." Stan quips as he eyes the empty bottle. "Don't mind if I do." He takes a Modelo from the fridge.

Olivia hands him a bottle opener. He pops the cap, then goes into the bedroom to see Pam.

"Hey, Pam. What's up?" He takes a swig.

"You're having a beer?" Pam sneers.

"Do I have your permission?" He sits in the chair by the bed.

"What's up with the 'Patagonia' jacket. Is it cold outside?"

"I needed roomy pockets." He mutters as he steals the remote control.

"Hey, I was watching that."

"'Say Yes to the Dress?' You're kidding. That ship has sailed." He mindlessly scrolls through the channels stopping on an old western.

Olivia enters the bedroom, flashing a faux grin. "Miss Pam, would you like dessert? I saw ice cream in the freezer."

"No, thank you. The fish tacos filled me up."

"Fish tacos?" Stan wines, with a pout.

"Yeah, you missed out." Pam says. "They were scrumptious."

Pam and Stan are expecting Olivia to go back to the kitchen. She doesn't. Instead, she slowly surveys the room, looking at the photographs and artwork on the walls. Pam and Stan stare at each other with wide eyed panic, both anticipating her next move.

Olivia stops at a photo of Pam with her daughter, granddaughter, and grandson at the beach.

"So cute." Olivia mumbles, as she glares at Pam. The kindness in her face melts, as her pupils enlarge. "I had a daughter." She stares at the closet door on the opposite wall, as if in a hypnotic trance. "She's gone."

Pam remains silent.

Stan blurts, "Where did she go?" Guzzling his beer, he leans forward, as if he's watching an action movie, awaiting the next fight scene.

"She's in heaven." Olivia is stoic, staring at the closet door.

Pam glares at Stan, signaling with her wide open eyes for him to shut up.

Stan gets the message.

"She had just turned four." Olivia turns her gaze to Pam and continues. "I was working that night. My boyfriend was supposed to be watching her. He had been sober for six months. His jerk-off friend came over with heroin."

Pam's eyes fill with moisture at the anticipation of the finale of the sad story.

Olivia resumes. "We lived in an apartment in Chula Vista. My boyfriend was so high, he was incoherent. Sasha went out the front door and decided to go swimming in the pool. She didn't know how to swim. It was dark. My neighbor found her, but it was too late."

"I am so sorry." Pam dots her nose with a tissue.

Olivia is motionless. "That was twelve years ago. It feels like yesterday."

"Of course, it would." Stan interrupts. "You never get over the loss of a child. I know from personal experience."

Pam turns to Stan. "You lost a child?" A tear trickles down his cheek, disappearing into his beard.

"He wasn't a child. He was a soldier. In Afghanistan."

"I'm so sorry, Stan." Pam says.

Olivia stares at him sympathetically.

"Enough of this sad crap." Stan addresses Olivia. "I can hang out with Pam until bedtime. You can go."

Olivia shoots him a malicious glare. "My job's not done." She straightens her posture, then pulls a tissue from her pocket and wipes her cheeks. "I can't leave before my shift is up."

"I'll be fine." Pam says optimistically, trying to uplift herself from the heartbreaking conversation. "Stan is going to stay with me for a while."

Stan nods in agreement.

"Maybe you didn't hear me." Olivia scowls at Pam. Her eyes emanate malevolence. "I have a job to do." She slides her hands into her pockets.

Pam hasn't had a chance to tell Stan what's in those pockets.

Olivia keeps her hands concealed for less than a minute, but it feels like an hour. Pam stares at her intently, awaiting her next move.

Finally, she pulls her hands out, touching her face, searching for any remaining tears. Then she goes into the bathroom, slamming the door.

"Now you know why she's crazy." Stan tells Pam.

"Yeah, but…is that an excuse for murdering innocent people?"

"What if you are way off base here, Pam?"

"I might be, but I can't take a chance. This is my life we're talking about. And yours! I need you to grab those needles out of the pockets of her lab coat."

"What needles?"

"There's one in each pocket! I was spying on her with my 'Blink' app."

"What's in them?"

"I don't know! She's going to shoot me up with some illicit drugs."

They hear the flush of the toilet. A moment later Olivia comes back into the bedroom.

"Mr. Stan, it's time for you to go now." She says firmly.

"I'm staying." He replies, with forced confidence. His stress level is mounting with each second. He pulls his shoulders back to feel taller. "You're the one who's leaving."

"I have to finish my shift." She stresses sternly.

"I will pay for your full shift." Pam interjects. "I won't

tell Beth you left early."

"I'm repeating myself. I'm not going anywhere until I finish my job." Flames ignite in her pupils. She takes two steps toward Pam who is sitting in bed, defenseless and vulnerable. Olivia's hands are hidden in the pockets of her lab coat.

Pam's engulfed in panic, unable to speak.

Stan stands. "Empty your pockets." He demands.

"You are a crazy old man." Olivia ignores his request, shaking her head.

"I said," his volume escalates, "empty your pockets." Stan looks up at her. He's not intimidated by her size.

"No." She pulls her shoulders back and glares at him.

"Take off your lab coat."

"You're losing it, old man. I'm not taking anything off for you."

Pam's witnessing this exchange. Her heart is palpitating. Sweat drizzles down her temples. *Olivia is going to punch him in the jaw and knock him out. Then I'll have to fend for myself!*

Stan is motionless. His hands are hidden in the pockets of his ski jacket. His cheeks are flushed. His eyes don't blink.

Olivia's hands are still stashed in the pockets of her lab coat. Pam sees her fingers fumbling inside the pockets. She's as still as a statue. Her brown eyes are blazing with anticipation.

Stan and Olivia are staring at each other intently, as though they're in an old west gunfight, itching to be the first to draw.

"Take your lab coat off!" Stan pulls his Glock handgun out of his left pocket and holds it with both hands, aimed at her chest. Trembling, the gun nearly slips out of his sweaty palms.

Her lips upturn slightly, forming a skeptical grin. Slowly and meticulously, she extracts her hands from her pockets, with her unblinking eyes glued on Stan. They're empty. She raises her arms above her shoulders.

"Hold on, crazy old man," she giggles. "What are you doing?"

"Take your coat off." He demands. His grip becomes razor steady.

"All right, all right." She gingerly removes the garment, holding it away from her body, hanging it on her index finger. The tight fit of her yellow polo shirt reveals her big breasts and stomach roll.

"Give it to Pam." Stan orders, taking a step back, not wanting to be too close for fear she'll grab his gun.

Olivia tosses it on the bed. "I'm getting out of here before you accidentally fire that dangerous thing. You don't even know how to use it." She turns to exit the room.

"Bang!"

Pam nearly jumps out of her skin as the ear-piercing boom vibrates the walls. *Did Stan shoot Olivia?* She closes her eyes as tight, afraid to open them. Her hands instinctively cover her mouth, minimizing her scream. A faint, burnt smell permeates her nostrils.

Cautiously, she uncovers her face, surveying the room.

Olivia is standing in the doorway, staring at Stan. Her eyes are fierce with determination. She crosses her arms across her chest like a fearless superhero.

"I know how to use this." Stan's tone is steady and resolute. "Do you want me to show you again?"

Olivia races out of the house, grabbing her purse and black bag off the chair. Stan goes into the dining room, watching raptly out the window. The roar of her mufflers rattles the glass. She backs up recklessly, then punches on the gas.

"Dammit! What just happened?" Pam shouts.

"I scared her away." Stan says as he enters the bedroom, puffing with pride.

"Is she going to report us to the police?"

"No way. She's a criminal herself. Are you okay?"

"I'm fine. I think." Pam says as she fluffs the pillows on her back. "What about you?"

"Couldn't be better. Sorry about the bullet hole in your ceiling."

Pam follows his gaze upward, noticing a small black hole in the ceiling above the doorway.

"Don't be sorry, you saved my life." She smiles.

Pam scrambles for the lab coat at the foot of the bed. She pulls out a hypodermic needle from the left pocket. Then another needle from the right.

"Don't touch those!" Stan shouts. "Her fingerprints are plastered all over them."

She shoves them back into the pocket, and gently rolls the garment into a tight bundle, with the needles protected in the center.

"Stan, put this in my laptop bag. We'll take it to the police tomorrow, along with the knife."

"Did you say we?" Stan raises one brow.

"Yes, you and me. And let's not mention this to John."

"Why?"

"Because he thinks I'm a paranoid busybody. I just don't want to explain all of this."

"With a hole in the ceiling, you might have to. When is he coming home?"

"Tomorrow, about five."

"Tell you what, I'll bring my drywall patch over in the morning and fix it. Do you have any paint for the ceiling?"

"Yeah, in the garage."

"Problem solved." Stan brushes his hands together as though drywall patching is entertaining.

CHAPTER FOURTEEN

At 8:00 a.m. Stan arrives with his ladder and drywall supplies to repair the bullet hole.

"As soon as you're done fixing that, I need you to drive me to police headquarters. I'm calling Detective Rossi to verify that he's available. Do detective's work Sundays?"

"Hell, if I know." Stan climbs the ladder to begin his patching. Pam hobbles to the bathroom to put on her makeup.

Emerging twenty minutes later, she's dressed in burgundy pants and a sleeveless, button-up floral blouse. She applied her makeup with precision and curled her hair. Stan is relaxing in the recliner, reading a cooking magazine.

"You're done?" Pam stares at the ceiling, examining Stan's handy work.

Stan gives her a once over. "You look nice."

Pam smiles. "Thanks."

He points at the ceiling. "That's just the first coat. I'll let it dry, then sand it before I put on the final coat."

"How long will that take?"

"An hour or so."

"Will you drive me to the police station now?"

"You're the boss." He gives her a military salute.

Stan helps Pam into his pickup.

"So, how often do you see your daughter and grandchildren in Escondido?" Pam asks.

"Not often enough. My daughter and son in law are busy. Work, kids' sports, all that."

"How old are your grandkids?"

"I have two grandsons. The oldest just turned thirteen, and his brother is ten."

"Fun ages."

"Debbie always coordinated our visits. Since she passed my daughter has told me, a couple of times, that I should sell the house and move closer."

"That's a great idea."

"I like my house." Stan pouts.

"Of course you do, but do you really need a home that big? Lot's of maintenance. I know it's a challenge to keep up with."

"The boys are growing so fast." Stan says with a tone of longing. "I gave them some old comic books I had." He smiles. "You would have thought they won the lottery when I gave them to them. They're good boys. Smart as whips."

"What a thoughtful gift."

He parks in the public lot adjacent to the station. "I'll wait here."

"Why? I thought you wanted to tell the police your wife wouldn't commit suicide?"

"I'm an absent-minded, old man. They don't care what I have to say."

"Are you sure?"

"Yeah, I'm sure." Stan fiddles with the radio. "That thing is for the Fitzgerald case." He points to the laptop bag on Pam's lap. "There is no Powalski case."

"Okay. I'll give him the dagger, and see what he says. I also have my iPad, so I can show him the video of Olivia when she was going to attack me with hypodermic needles."

"Don't show him that." Stan exclaims.

"Why not?"

"Because I shot first."

"It was self-defense."

"The detective may not see it that way." He shakes his head. "Remember, I'm a delusional old man."

"No, you're not." She punches him playfully in the arm.

"Okay, I'll hold off telling him about that, and about the surveillance footage Peter gathered. But I've got to know what's in those needles. This killer must be stopped!"

As Pam approaches the entrance a young police officer steps past her to open the glass doors. He takes her lap top bag so she can maneuver her crutches. She slowly enters the lobby. Policemen in crisp uniforms are coming and going. She detects the aroma of fresh brewed coffee mixed with men's cologne.

Pam stands before the receptionist, whose talking on the phone behind plexiglass. She waits patiently for her to finish her conversation. The receptionist writes down Pam's name and requests that she take a seat. After waiting about ten minutes, she gives Pam directions to Detective Rossi's office at the end of the corridor.

Entering cautiously, Pam notices numerous framed certificates on the wall. The detective stands to greet her. With his friendly smile, and disheveled long brown hair, he's not what Pam expected. Much younger and casual with his untucked, short-sleeved shirt and faded jeans. And handsome.

"Hello, I'm Detective Rossi." He shakes Pam's hand, then points to the chair opposite his desk.

"I'm Pam Guerrero. You may know my husband, John Guerrero. He retired about five years ago from the SDPD."

"I transferred here from Los Angeles four years ago. I've heard of him. He's a legend around here."

"Yeah, a legend in his own mind," Pam jokes. "You and I talked about three weeks ago. I called you when I found a knife in my neighborhood."

"I remember. You never showed up. I left you a message."

"I got your message. I was delayed. Unfortunately, I was in a car accident."

"Sorry to hear that." He gazes at the crutches leaning on his desk. "Are you okay?"

"Hobbling a bit, but I will be fine. I broke a couple of bones in my foot."

"That doesn't sound fun." He smiles warmly.

Pam pulls the plastic bag out of her laptop bag and hands it to him. "I found this when I was walking my dog."

He opens it, staring at the weapon. Next, he carefully extracts it, holding the handle with his fingertips. Flipping it over for further examination, he sets it on the plastic bag. He jots notes on his legal pad.

"Is that dried blood on it?" Pam asks. "Can you extract DNA from it?"

"Most likely. I'm not sure until the lab finishes their analysis. Where did you find this?"

"I was walking my dog along the bike path adjacent to La Jolla Boulevard. I sited a shiny object under the oak leaves. I'm not a weapons expert, but I think this dagger is the one missing from Marvin Fitzgerald's collection. The Fitzgerald's are longtime friends of mine. Or, I should say, were." *The detective doesn't need to know Beth precipitated the demise of her and John's crumbling marriage.*

The detective takes more notes.

"Beth is so distraught that no suspects have been found

in her husband's murder." Pam says. "Or do you have one?"

"There are a few leads that were following, but nothing conclusive. If this is the knife missing from his collection, this will help immensely. I'll test this for DNA." He stands, signaling their meeting is ending. "I appreciate you're bringing this in."

"Wait, I have more information."

He sits back in his chair, glancing at his watch.

"A home health worker came to my house." She pulls the lab coat out of her bag. "Can you please check out these two hypodermic needles? They must contain a lethal dose of something. And I have video of her filling the vials and hiding them in her pockets. She was going to kill me!"

"What does this have to do with the Marvin Fitzgerald case?"

Pam leans forward, planting her elbows on his desk.

"There have been four deaths in my neighborhood in four months" Pam holds up four fingers. "That's not a coincidence."

"Actually, it could be. Ms. Guerrero, serial killers are very rare." Detective Rossi says.

"You sound like my husband." Pam utters under her breath. "Marvin's was the first murder. These hypodermic needles may have nothing to do with it, or there may be a link. I don't know."

"What would be her motive for killing you?"

"What was her motive for murdering my neighbors? Do serial killers ever have a motive?"

"Let me get the knife and the needles tested. We will take it from there." He stands. "Thank you for your assistance."

"Then what?"

"I'll be in touch."

"How long does it take to obtain the results?"

"Seventy-two hours."

CHAPTER FIFTEEN

Three days later, John goes to Beth's house to paint her family room. Pam has been married to John long enough to know that when he starts a job he has to finish. He'll be there all day. Pam is so over him; she can't even conceive why she still shares his bed. Well right now she isn't, because she sleeps downstairs. For now, her excuse for staying is having a broken foot.

Pam takes an Uber, and arrives at Detective Rossi's office exactly seventy-two hours after their meeting. She's expecting to be brushed off as a nosy neighbor, but instead he is cordial and attentive.

"What did you find out about the knife?" Pam is eager for his answer.

"Please sit down, Ms. Guerrero. What you have provided is a crucial piece of evidence. Thank you for submitting it to us. Often private citizens resist involvement. We could solve more crimes with community cooperation."

"Glad I could help." Pam says.

"What I'm about to tell you is highly confidential. And the only reason I' giving you these details, is because I feel you are in a position to help the investigation even further."

"I don't know what you're talking about, but well okay.

I'm always willing to help if I can." Pam says cheerfully.

"The blood on the knife belonged to Marvin Fitzgerald." His expression is stoic and void of emotion

"I knew it!" Pam leans back and exhales a dramatic sigh, as if she's solved the crime of the century.

"What's equally important are the fingerprints on the handle." The detective says.

She leans forward. "Whose are they?"

"When a homicide occurs, everyone who had contact with the victim is considered a suspect. The fingerprints belong to an employee of 'Sunset Heath'. The caretaker who found Professor Fitzgerald in his office. She has a criminal record, and has served time for drug dealing, robbery and murder."

Pam's thoughts are jumbled. She has a vision of Marvin, in happier times, sitting by his backyard pool. "Did you say murder?"

"Yes. She killed her boyfriend, and served twelve years for the crime. Her name is Amy Landsburg."

"The Ford pickup I rear ended on the freeway was driven by Lance Landsburg! I saw his name on the police report. Could they be related?"

He writes notes on his pad. "We'll check into it."

"Does she also go by Olivia Jones?" Pam asks.

"I'm not aware that she does. We will find out when we apprehend her."

"She's the one." Pam points at the detective. "The mystery woman I saw on the videos!"

"What videos?" His brows converge.

Pam explains that with the help of a computer student at UCSD, she viewed the surveillance recordings of the four residences where a death occurred, and that a stocky woman with long brown hair, wearing a light blue lab coat was the common thread.

"And then she came to my house!" Pam exclaims. "She was going to kill me by lethal injection."

"Don't hypothesize conclusions, Mrs. Guerrero. There could be no correlation."

"Did you find out what was contained in those hypodermic needles I brought you?"

"One hundred milligrams of sodium phenobarbital."

"What is sodium phenobarbital?"

"A sedative often used to calm seizures. The cumulative dosage in the needles was sufficient to cause the heart and respiratory systems to slow considerably, possibly resulting in death, depending on the health and size of the person."

"I told you; she was going to kill me!"

"I'll ask the judge to issue a warrant for the video footage from each of the homes where a death occurred. Can you provide the addresses?"

"Yes, I have them right here." She extracts her leather clad notebook from her purse.

He overlooks the fact Pam had no authority to hack into the Johnson's and Fitzgerald's security cameras.

"Perhaps the video will supply more evidence implicating that Ms. Landsburg was involved in more than just the Marvin Fitzgerald incident."

"Incident! You mean murder. That woman is an assassin!"

"Mrs. Guerrero, at this point I must assume there is no correlation in the deaths, until substantial evidence proves otherwise. I must reiterate, this case is highly confidential." He sits on the desk, looking down at Pam. "We can arrest Amy Landsburg based on the fingerprint match, but we are not releasing any information to the press until we obtain more evidence. Please don't mention our conversation to anyone. Not even your husband. It could impede the investigation."

"My lips are sealed. You can trust me."

CHAPTER SIXTEEN

As Pam and John are eating brunch, Pam receives a phone call from Detective Rossi.

"I have a few more questions regarding the Fitzgerald murder case. Can you come to headquarters?"

"Sure. I'll be there thirty minutes, or so." Click.

"Who was that?" John demands, in an offensive tone.

"My boyfriend." Pam states confidently as she grabs her crutches.

"What the hell!" His face flushes beet red with anger.

"You have a girlfriend, so why can't I have a boyfriend?" She says with unwavering steadiness. "I know about you and Beth."

Pam goes into the guest room to get her purse. John trails her through the family room.

"And, I want a divorce." She announces calmly as she closes the bedroom door in his face, eliminating John's opportunity for rebuttal.

She hears John footsteps ascending the stairs. She calls Uber for a ride then goes out front to sit on the bench on the front landing to wait for the driver.

John appears a moment later. "Where are you going?"

He says with a clenched jaw and flushed cheeks.

"I told you already." A black Honda Accord pulls up in front of the house. The driver sees Pam using crutches, so he quickly comes up the walk to assist. Pam hobbles to the car. The driver puts her purse, and crutch, in the trunk. Then he helps her into the back seat.

"I won't be here when you get back." John shouts.

"Whatever." Pam says in a smart-ass tone. "Where are you going?"

"Vegas." John's son from his first marriage lives in Henderson.

The driver closes the car door. John can't see Pam behind the smoked glass, but she can see him. He stares at the vehicle with an angry grimace until it's out of sight.

John storms into the house, and throws some clothes into his suitcase. He goes into the garage to retrieve the knife, which he had planned to clean up and sell it at a pawn shop in Las Vegas. He digs through his tool box, lifting the small tools. He knows exactly where he stashed the white plastic bag. *It's gone! Dammit, Pam found it!*

Detective Rossi explains that he's disclosing more than he would in a typical case because he needs Pam's help. Amy Landsburg confessed to killing Marvin Fitzgerald, and burying the murder weapon under a tree. Amy Landsburg is arrested at her San Diego apartment without incident.

"Mrs. Landsburg is pleading for clemency. This is a murder for hire situation, Mrs. Guerrero. She is willing to testify against her boss in exchange for a lesser charge."

"Her boss?" Pam can't believe what she's hearing. Thoughts of Marvin, Richard Johnson, Debbie Powalski, and Fernando Ortiz Sr. flood her brain. The conversations of the last few months, the details, the videos, the tragedies. "Did you say, her boss? Her boss is my friend, Beth Fitzgerald." *Not only is Beth, my so- called friend, and an adulterer, she's also an assassin?*

"I'm well aware, which is why I asked you to come in to see me. We were able to confirm through researching the video surveillance footage, that each time a camera was disabled, the command came from Ms. Fitzgerald's cell phone. Amy Landsburg was her puppet. Her hitman. Mrs. Fitzgerald paid her generously."

"What?" Pam's eyes widen in disbelief. Her stomach churns in pre-vomit mode. She takes a gulp of coffee. "This is unreal."

"Beth Fitzgerald is the mastermind behind numerous, shall we say, planned deaths in San Diego County. I need irrefutable evidence to arrest her. The testimony of a convicted felon is not ironclad."

Pam stares at Detective Rossi, in shock. *Beth is a cold-blooded killer? How could she be two people at once? It's like she has a split personality.*

"Mrs. Guerrero, you seem like you could be persuasive." Detective Rossi states in his soothing, convincing baritone voice.

"I guess I can when I want to be." Pam responds.

"Can you get a confession from Beth Fitzgerald?"

Pam pauses, analyzing the difficulty of the task. "I'm not sure, I mean, I'll try."

"Would you be willing to wear a wire?"

"Like in the movies?" Pam's eyes light up as memories of writing salacious stories early in her career pop into her brain.

"Yes. If she confesses to the crimes, I can arrest her. An admission of guilt to a friend, as opposed to one to a detective, is often viewed upon more favorably by a jury. Detectives have been accused of coercing confessions."

"I get it. I've watched the 'Innocence Files'."

"I know you live three houses down from the Fitzgerald residence."

Pam nods.

"I'll wait at your house." He continues. "I'll be listening to every word. If you can get a confession out of her, I'll arrest her on the spot."

"I can do it, Detective Rossi." Pam puffs up her chest "I won't let you down."

"I appreciate your cooperation. Time is critical. If Beth Fitzgerald gets word that we've arrested Amy Landsburg, she may be a flight risk. How about tomorrow?"

"That should work. She is usually home on Saturdays, and my husband is out of town."

"I'll be at your house at 9:00 a.m."

CHAPTER SEVENTEEN

Pam wakes up at five, unable to sleep. She eats a protein breakfast of scrambled eggs and cheese to sustain herself for the stressful task she's about to undertake. She curls her gray locks and applies her makeup perfectly. Then she slips on her black leggings and favorite multi colored tunic. *I've got to look good for that handsome detective.* She's ready at eight, fifty minutes before Detective Rossi arrives.

Watching out the window, Pam sees him pull into her driveway in an unmarked sedan. She opens the door as he approaches.

"Good morning." Pam motions for him to enter.

His eyes wander the walls of the formal living room, and to the long dining table with its beautiful multiple centerpieces.

"You have a lovely home, Mrs. Guerrero."

"Thank you." She smiles. "Please call me Pam."

"You seem to be walking better." He looks down at her feet. "Just one crutch?"

"I got this fancy orthopedic boot yesterday."

"Um, styling." He follows her into the dining room.

"I'm guessing you've never worn a wire before."

"Good guess."

"It's really quite simple." He reaches in his brown leather satchel. "You wear this small microphone, discreetly. Attached to your bra would be an ideal location." He hands her a small item that resembles a large button wrapped in black mesh. It has a clip attached. "It's wireless. I'll be here with the transmitter."

Pam reaches into her vee neck blouse and attaches the microphone to her bra, in the middle of her breasts, well hidden by her blouse.

"Perfect." Detective Rossi says. He places an earpiece in his ear. "I'll be listening to every word of your conversation. Leave the front door is unlocked after you enter. I'll be at the Fitzgerald residence in less than a minute if she tries anything. Are you sure you're not in danger?"

"I'll whack her with my crutch." Pam says with a nervous chuckle. "She won't try anything. She doesn't have the guts. Her employee is doing her dirty work."

Pam takes a deep breath as she stands, checking her image in the mirror. Wiping the sweat from her brow, she psyches herself up for the stressful meeting with her ex-friend. *Coercing a confession is foreign territory.*

Detective Rossi follows her to the door.

"Wish me luck." Pam declares with forced cheerfulness.

"You don't need it. You can do this." He gives her a thumbs up.

With the walking boot Pam can almost walk without the crutch. She stuffs the crutch under her arm for extra security, and possibly protection. She waddles down the sidewalk, with thoughts swirling in her brain like a pinwheel. *I thought I knew Beth, but she deceived me. I can't believe she's an assassin. And John is nothing but a liar and a cheater. Who can I trust anymore?*

She rings Beth's doorbell. Inhaling deeply, she calms her nerves.

Beth opens the door slowly. "Hi, Pam." She seems surprised by the visit. "How are you?"

"Fine." Pam blurts.

"Look at you walking! You look great." Beth says perkily.

"Thanks."

"What's up?"

"Not much. How...how are you?" Pam stutters. She never stutters. Her nerves are like a jumble of crisscrossed, tangled wires. She smiles, attempting to hide her distress.

"Come in." Beth waves her hand in butler mode.

Pam enters the foyer, careful to leave the front door unlocked when she closes it.

"Would you like a cup of coffee?"

"Yes, please."

Pam sits on the couch. She glances at the armpits of her floral silk blouse noticing sweat stains. She inhales and exhales methodically, calming herself.

Beth returns with hot mugs, setting them on coasters on the coffee table. She sits on the opposite end of the couch. Pam takes a gulp and clears her throat. She's at a loss for words. An unusual position for her.

Beth breaks the unnerving silence. "How is your foot?"

"Much better. The walking boot really helps."

"And, how are the grandkids?"

"They're fine. I plan on visiting Texas as soon as my foot heals. Beth, I'm actually here to talk about something else."

Beth leans back and crosses her legs. Her expression becomes grim, as her red lips purse malevolently. Her hazel eyes squint with an aura of deceitfulness.

Pam stares at her, sensing her own eyes filling with

anger. Taking another deep breath, she collects her nerves.

"I know what you did." She blurts.

Beth's cheeks flush crimson as she searches for words.

"It wasn't my fault, Pam." She declares, defensively. "Believe me, it was John. He's always flirted with me. After Marvin got sick, he consoled me."

"Oh, all John's fault, uh?" Pam says in a smart-ass tone.

"I was vulnerable, I guess." She reaches to pat Pam's thigh. "I didn't mean to hurt you. It just happened."

"I don't care about how long you've been having an affair with my husband." Pam is calm and methodical. "I'm divorcing him. That is trivial compared to what else you did."

"What do you mean?" she asks, feigning innocence.

"Your actions are so hard for me to comprehend. I know your secret."

Beth's eyebrows converge in a vee. "What secret?"

Pam pulls her head back, like a cobra recoiling before a strike. "You're busted, Beth. You disabled the surveillance cameras each time a death occurred in the neighborhood. Your employee, Amy Landsburg, or Olivia, whatever her name is, is an ex-felon who killed her boyfriend, so had no qualms about being paid to do away with strangers. You paid her generously."

"What are you talking about, Pam? You need to get off your pain medication."

Pam stands, pointing her finger at Beth. "You did it! You killed Marvin! And Richard Johnson. And Debbie Powalski. And Fernando Ortiz! And you thought about killing me! Why? Why, Beth? Why did you do it?"

Beth stares at Pam. The beauty of her hazel eyes is replaced by an evil shamelessness. Her perfect pale complexion turns ruddy, as if her blood is boiling in her body. She slowly stands, and moves toward the French doors framing her lush back yard and serene pool.

"Death is personal." She utters, in a monotone.

"What the hell are you talking about?" Pam grabs a tissue and blots the sweat from her temple.

"I provide a service." Beth continues. "A much-needed service."

Pam crosses her arms across her chest. "I don't understand."

"Mr. Ortiz, for example. He was ready to go. A textbook case, actually" She smiles as if she's reminiscing a pleasant memory. "I wish all my cases were like his."

"What's that supposed to mean?" Pam shakes her head.

"He paid to receive a lethal injection. He didn't want to burden his family with seeing him die a slow death from cancer, or chemo treatments, whatever got him first. He had pancreatic cancer."

"He paid you to kill him?" Pam is astonished at Beth's explanation.

"Euthanasia. If it's good enough for our beloved pets, why shouldn't it be good enough for us humans?"

"And Richard Johnson. Why him? He was my friend."

"Who?"

"Richard Johnson. He lived one street over. He had an aneurysm."

"I had nothing to do with that." Beth states defensively.

"What about Mrs. Powalski? What was her story? If she wanted to kill herself, why didn't she just take a bunch of pills? Who shoots themselves? Really, how did you think that would not be suspicious?"

Beth is cool and composed, like she's imparting a philosophical theory. "I comply with my client's requests. Debbie Powalski wanted to make her husband feel guilty. Like he shot her with his own gun." She shrugs her shoulders. "I don't know why she was so intent on getting back at him. He obviously did something that pissed her off. It was none of my business. I'm not a counselor. I'm a problem solver."

"You're an assassin! That's what you are! And insane. Where do you find these so-called clients?"

"They find me."

"And why would you have your own husband stabbed? That is so horrific."

"Marvin loved his knives. And he hated having Parkinson's. You didn't live with him, Pam. You didn't know what it was like. The suffering he was experiencing. That's the way he would have wanted to go."

"Did you ask him?"

"I didn't have to." Beth gazes at a photo of her and Marvin hanging on the wall. They're standing by the pool, smiling broadly. Pam remembers it was taken at their forty-fifth anniversary party. "He's at peace now."

"And why did you instruct your employee to inject me with drugs? Why did you want to do away with me?"

"That was John's idea." She pauses, using her words wisely. "He thought it was easier than divorce."

"Easier? That asshole." Pam shakes her head. "You mean more economically beneficial. You are sick, Beth."

Their intense conversation is interrupted by the creak of the front door hinge. They glare at each other.

Beth glances toward the foyer. "I'm not expecting anyone."

"I am." Pam replies confidently.

Detective Rossi enters the living room. Beth glares at him, and then at Pam.

"You set me up." Beth scowls at Pam.

"You set yourself up." Detective Rossi states as he slides handcuffs on her delicate wrists and recites her Miranda rights.

EPILOGUE

Amy Landsburg was found guilty of murder for the death of Marvin Fitzgerald and Debbie Powalski. Her fingerprints were found on both the dagger, and Stan's gun.

She was also found guilty of the murder of Richard Johnson. Laura Johnson had paid Beth big bucks to arrange the exchange of her husband's blood pressure medicine for a high dose of Ofloxacin. Amy carried out Beth's instructions. Beth's greed overrode her mission of helping those who are suffering from life threatening illnesses make decisions about their own destiny. Richard Johnson did not make the choice to end his life. Laura Johnson did.

Charges against Amy in the death of Fernando Ortiz were dropped due to lack of evidence.

Amy's sentence was reduced to ten years in exchange for her testimony against Beth Fitzgerald.

Lance Landsburg was charged with reckless , and inciting the accident that caused Pam Guerrero's injuries. Funds were traced proving Beth paid Amy's husband a sizable sum to ensure Pam never arrived at the police station with the evidence.

Stan Powalski sold his house and bought a townhouse in a gated retirement community in Escondido, near his daughter and her family. His wife had never forgiven him for encouraging their son to join the army. His daughter didn't blame him for her brother's choices.

Pam divorced John, sold her house, and relocated to Austin to be near her daughter and her grandchildren. She and Stan have maintained their friendship via email.

John moved in with Beth, and is now her pool boy, gardener and personal gigolo. Beth took the wrap for John's conspiracy charge by claiming she lied when she told Pam that eliminating her via lethal injection was John's idea.

Beth Fitzgerald was implicated in nine murders in San Diego County, and charged with conspiracy to commit murder in the first degree. She hired a high dollar lawyer to get her off, professing her innocence, declaring she's an angel of death, another Dr. Kevorkian. Her creative attorney has been dragging the proceedings on for years.

In Beth Fitzgerald's twisted mind, her actions were mercy killings, claiming those who died under her direction, requested the outcome. She's being heralded a hero by 'Death With Dignity 'advocates.

Only the dead victims, who have been forever silenced, could reveal the truth. Death is indeed personal.

ABOUT THE AUTHOR

Sally Dallas writes romantic crime thrillers, cozy mysteries, and historical fiction, available exclusively on Amazon. Learn more about her at sallydallas.com.

Please write a review for *Death is Personal* on Amazon.